Agent Mongoose
and the
Hypno-Beam Scheme

Dan Jolley

illustrated by Matt Wendt

GRAPHIC UNIVERSE™ · MINNEAPOLIS · NEW YORK

Story by Dan Jolley

Pencils and inks by Matt Wendt

Coloring by Hi-Fi Design

Lettering by Marshall Dillon

Copyright © 2009 by Lerner Publishing Group, Inc.

Graphic Universe™ is a trademark and Twisted Journeys® is a registered trademark of Lerner Publishing Group, Inc.

Graphic Universe
A division of Lerner Publishing Group, Inc.
241 First Avenue North
Minneapolis, MN 55401 U.S.A.

Website address: www.lernerbooks.com

Library of Congress Cataloging-in-Publication Data

Jolley, Dan.
    Agent Mongoose and the hypno-beam scheme / by Dan Jolley ; illustrated by Matt Wendt.
        p.   cm.—(Twisted journeys)
    Summary: As the hero of this graphic novel whose top-secret mission is to follow an international trail of spies and foil the plans of an evil mastermind, the reader's choices determine the outcome of the story.
    ISBN: 978-0-8225-6203-0 (lib. bdg. : alk. paper)
    1. Plot-your-own stories. 2. Graphic novels. [1. Graphic novels. 2. Spies—Fiction.
3. Adventure and adventurers—Fiction. 4. Plot-your-own stories.] I. Wendt, Matt, ill. II. Title.
    PZ7.7.J65Ag 2009
    [Fic]—dc22   2008029150

Manufactured in the United States of America
1 2 3 4 5 6 – DP – 14 13 12 11 10 09

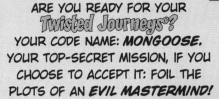

ARE YOU READY FOR YOUR *Twisted Journeys*®? YOUR CODE NAME: **MONGOOSE.** YOUR TOP-SECRET MISSION, IF YOU CHOOSE TO ACCEPT IT: FOIL THE PLOTS OF AN *EVIL MASTERMIND!*

EACH PAGE TELLS WHAT HAPPENS TO YOU AS YOU FOLLOW AN INTERNATIONAL TRAIL OF SPIES. YOUR WORDS AND THOUGHTS ARE SHOWN IN THE *YELLOW BALLOONS.* AND *YOU* GET TO DECIDE HOW TO OUTWIT YOUR FOES. JUST FOLLOW THE NOTE AT THE BOTTOM OF EACH PAGE UNTIL YOU REACH A *Twisted Journeys*® PAGE. THEN MAKE THE CHOICE *YOU* LIKE BEST.

BUT BE CAREFUL . . . THE WRONG CHOICE COULD MAKE YOUR MISSION *VERY SHORT!*

"Code name: Mongoose, reporting for duty," you say as you walk into Miss Worthington's office at the Agency. Her name isn't really Miss Worthington, but you don't know what her real name is. You've been an Agency spy for years, but you've never known her true identity.

"You're late," she snaps. "Sit down and pay attention."

You take a seat. "What's wrong this time? Death ray satellite? Mutant manatees? Someone contaminating the world's supply of pizza?"

"Focus, Mongoose. It's Dr. Van Horst again. And this time, he means business."

Now you *are* paying attention. Dr. Santiago Van Horst is as bad as they come—an evil genius determined to throw the whole planet into chaos and madness.

"Just tell me where he is and what you need me to do about it."

Miss Worthington narrows her eyes at you briefly before dimming the lights and starting a slide show. "Listen carefully."

4

GO ON TO THE NEXT PAGE.

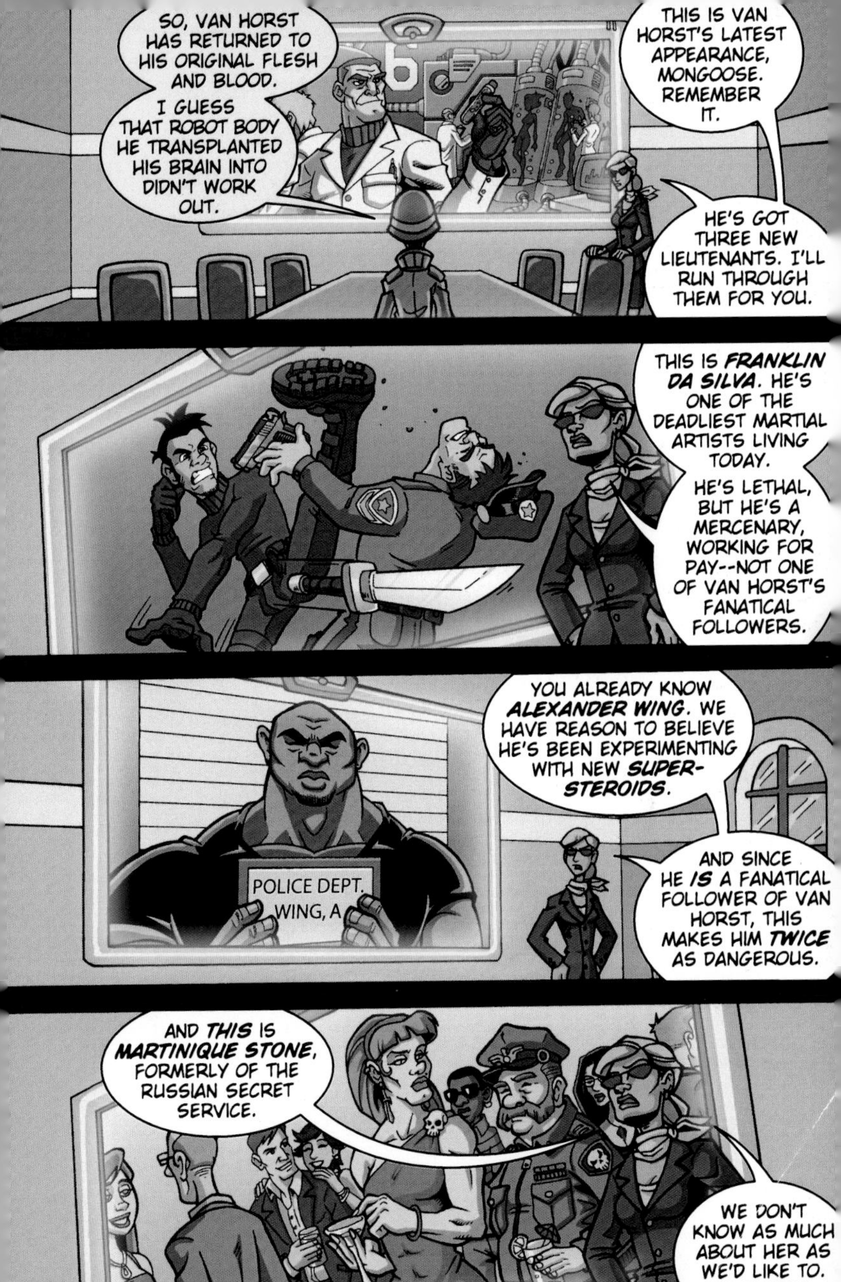
SO, VAN HORST HAS RETURNED TO HIS ORIGINAL FLESH AND BLOOD.
I GUESS THAT ROBOT BODY HE TRANSPLANTED HIS BRAIN INTO DIDN'T WORK OUT.
THIS IS VAN HORST'S LATEST APPEARANCE, MONGOOSE. REMEMBER IT.
HE'S GOT THREE NEW LIEUTENANTS. I'LL RUN THROUGH THEM FOR YOU.
THIS IS *FRANKLIN DA SILVA*. HE'S ONE OF THE DEADLIEST MARTIAL ARTISTS LIVING TODAY.
HE'S LETHAL, BUT HE'S A MERCENARY, WORKING FOR PAY--NOT ONE OF VAN HORST'S FANATICAL FOLLOWERS.
YOU ALREADY KNOW *ALEXANDER WING*. WE HAVE REASON TO BELIEVE HE'S BEEN EXPERIMENTING WITH NEW *SUPER-STEROIDS*.
POLICE DEPT. WING, A
AND SINCE HE *IS* A FANATICAL FOLLOWER OF VAN HORST, THIS MAKES HIM *TWICE* AS DANGEROUS.
AND *THIS* IS *MARTINIQUE STONE*, FORMERLY OF THE RUSSIAN SECRET SERVICE.
WE DON'T KNOW AS MUCH ABOUT HER AS WE'D LIKE TO. BE CAREFUL.

"Okay," you say, impatient to get going. "But what're they *doing*? Why did you bring me in?"

"We've narrowed it down to two possible objectives." Miss Worthington plants her hands on her desk and leans forward. Her eyes drill into yours. "Either one would spell catastrophe if Van Horst succeeds. You *cannot* fail, Mongoose."

"And I can't *succeed* unless you tell me what's going on!"

"Van Horst is either going to overthrow the world's most powerful countries through the use of hypnotic beams broadcast through television signals . . . or he's going to use a long-distance electromagnetic-pulse blaster to shut down all of the planet's technology."

"No way! We've gotta stop him! Where do I start?" You know just which special gizmos and gadgets you'll bring along.

She smiles grimly. "You have two options. We think he's researching the hypno-beam in Alaska. The EMP blaster, we believe, is being built in Paris, France."

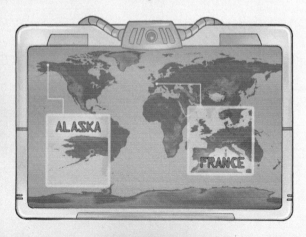

WILL YOU . . .

. . . head north to the last frontier?
TURN TO PAGE 16.

. . . hop a transatlantic flight and
brush up on your French?
TURN TO PAGE 42.

MIGHT AS WELL TAKE THESE IN ORDER. SO, FIRST ON THE LIST...

...IS A *JUNGLE*.

HUH. YOU DON'T SEE ANY TROPICAL BIRDS OR MONKEYS OR ANYTHING LIKE THAT.

BUT YOU *DO* FIND SOMETHING A LOT MORE *VALUABLE*.

HELP! HELP US!

GET US OUT OF HERE!

ARE YOU GUYS OKAY?

VAN HORST KIDNAPPED US AND FORCED US TO WORK ON ALL HIS CRAZY PROJECTS!

8

GO ON TO THE NEXT PAGE.

"Come on, move it!" you hiss at the scientists. "I don't know how long we've got!"

The men and women follow you back to the main dome, where you usher them up the ladder toward the ceiling. One of them mentions along the way that there's an escape craft up there, *just* big enough to hold the group.

It's incredibly tense as all of you make your way up toward the ceiling and through the hatch. And then suddenly a chorus of shouts breaks out from below you! You look down and see a dozen heavily armed mercenaries come rushing into the dome—and behind them is Van Horst himself.

You know they can't shoot at you. They wouldn't risk rupturing the dome. But they start climbing up after you and they're moving a lot faster than the scientists!

TURN TO PAGE 31.

There's a strange *whooshing* sound in your ears, and very abruptly, you find yourself standing in . . .

. . . you're not sure *what* you're standing in. You look around slowly.

You're inside an *underwater dome*. You might be on the bottom of the ocean!

There's a ladder leading up to a hatch in the ceiling and some kind of structure up there, outside the dome. Plus there's a hatch in the floor. But besides the hatches, the dome is *filled* with super-high-tech equipment. From the looks of this place, the hypno-beam and the electromagnetic-pulse blaster might *both* be around here somewhere.

Suddenly a voice you recognize booms out over an intercom. It's Van Horst himself.

"So, you've found my lair, have you, Mongoose? Well, it won't do you any good. You're not getting out of here alive."

10

GO ON TO THE NEXT PAGE.

This place is incredibly important—no one's ever found Van Horst's lair before! But what do you do now that you're here?

WILL YOU . . .

. . . climb the ladder to the hatch at the top of the dome?
TURN TO PAGE 34.

. . . look around at the equipment and try to identify your targets?
TURN TO PAGE 28.

. . . go through the hatch in the floor?
TURN TO PAGE 99.

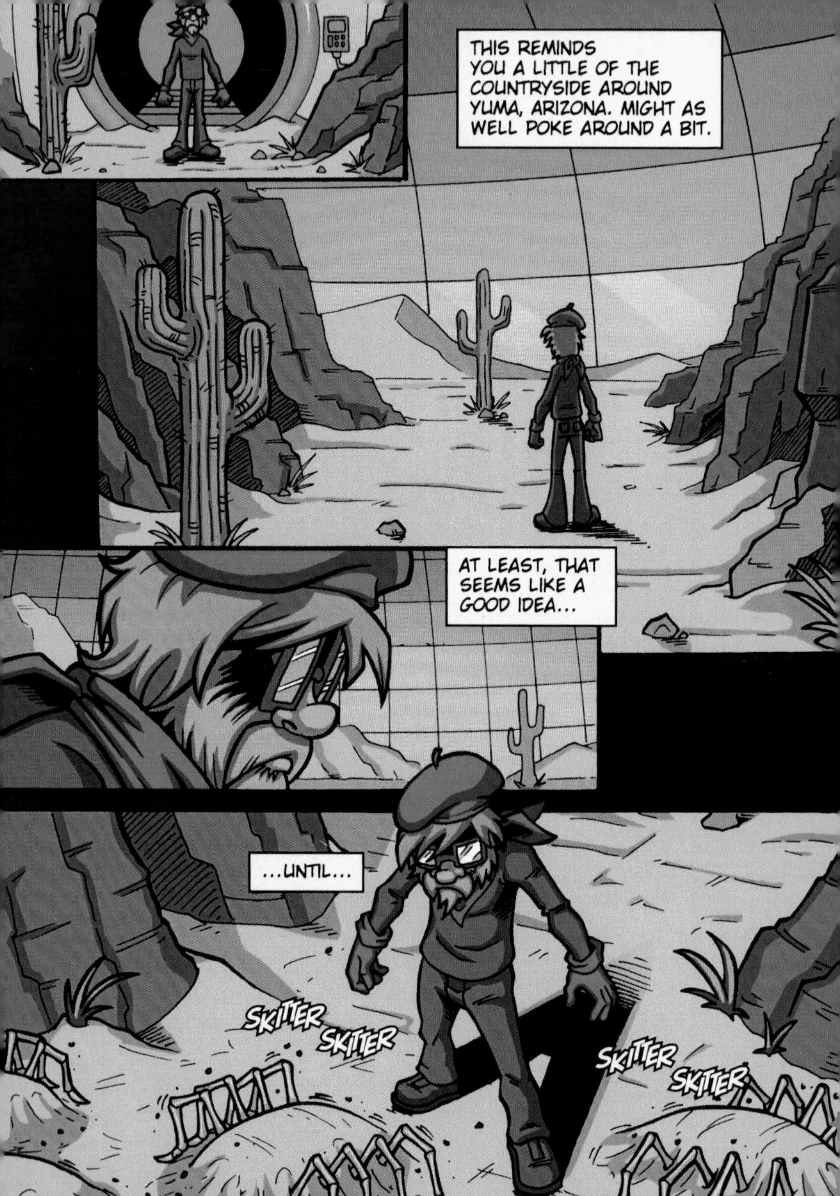
THIS REMINDS YOU A LITTLE OF THE COUNTRYSIDE AROUND YUMA, ARIZONA. MIGHT AS WELL POKE AROUND A BIT.
AT LEAST, THAT SEEMS LIKE A GOOD IDEA...
...UNTIL...
SKITTER SKITTER
SKITTER SKITTER

The rustling under the sand gets louder and louder . . . and suddenly the ground erupts! All around you, horrible, hissing creatures crawl up onto the surface.

They're *spiders*. And every one of them is at least three feet wide.

Van Horst's voice booms out of an unseen loudspeaker. "I see you've met my desert spiders, Mongoose," he chuckles. "I had you in mind specifically while I was breeding them. Hope you don't mind if they have you for dinner?"

The spiders scuttle closer, and you spin around and dash back toward the door . . .

. . . which closes and locks just as you reach it.

The spiders get closer . . . and closer . . . and when they're near enough for you to count all six of the loathsome eyes on each one of them, you know that the story of Code name: Mongoose has finally come to its conclusion.

THE END

You creep down a dank hallway. The hallway stops at a rectangular room—and at the room's far end, you can see a woman tied up with ropes, propped against the wall. She's not moving . . . but as you get closer, you think you recognize her. It's Martinique Stone! Why is she tied up? Has Van Horst turned on her?

She still doesn't move, but you hear another whimpering cry. It's definitely coming from her.

"We've got to help her!" Dolph whispers, standing at your left shoulder.

"I don't know," Eva murmurs from your right side. She sounds skeptical. "This feels like a trap."

You don't want to leave Martinique
Stone tied up if she's really in trouble . . .
but she's one of Van Horst's people!

WILL YOU . . .

. . . take a chance and go untie her?
TURN TO PAGE 23.

. . . decide she's on her own and get
back to your assignment?
TURN TO PAGE 58.

The Agency plane lands at a small, remote airstrip in Alaska many hours later. You know the summers here are beautiful and mild . . . but it's the dead of winter right now. You put on your custom-designed Arctic gear and get off the plane.

Winds howl, and the snow almost blinds you. You can barely see to make your way across the tarmac to the control tower. You discover it's nice and warm inside the building, but you're still cold enough to keep your gear on.

Your contact is a wiry, weasel-like man that you know only as Code name: Ziggurat. The two of you are the only people there at the moment.

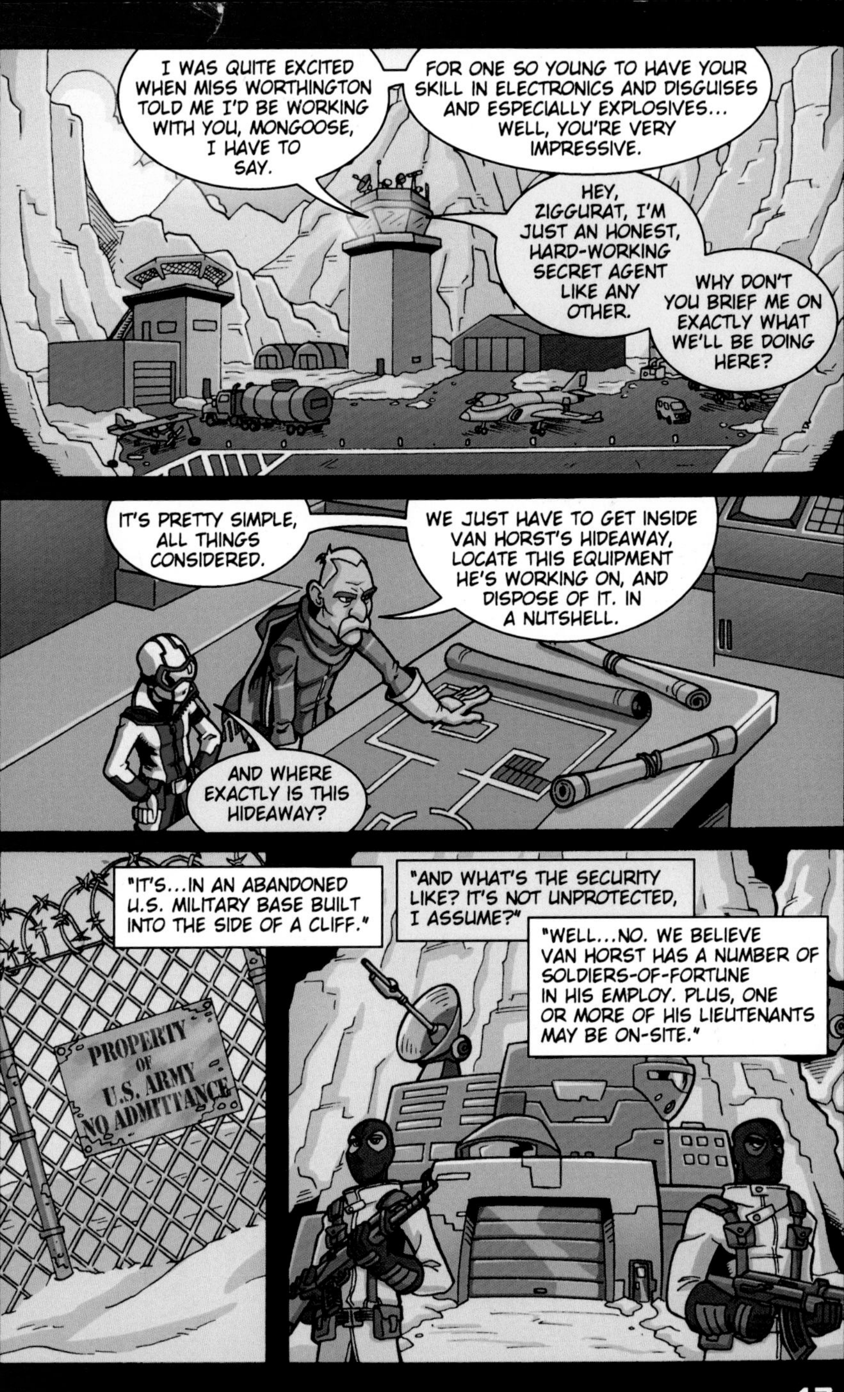
I WAS QUITE EXCITED WHEN MISS WORTHINGTON TOLD ME I'D BE WORKING WITH YOU, MONGOOSE, I HAVE TO SAY.
FOR ONE SO YOUNG TO HAVE YOUR SKILL IN ELECTRONICS AND DISGUISES AND ESPECIALLY EXPLOSIVES... WELL, YOU'RE VERY IMPRESSIVE.
HEY, ZIGGURAT, I'M JUST AN HONEST, HARD-WORKING SECRET AGENT LIKE ANY OTHER.
WHY DON'T YOU BRIEF ME ON EXACTLY WHAT WE'LL BE DOING HERE?
IT'S PRETTY SIMPLE, ALL THINGS CONSIDERED.
WE JUST HAVE TO GET INSIDE VAN HORST'S HIDEAWAY, LOCATE THIS EQUIPMENT HE'S WORKING ON, AND DISPOSE OF IT. IN A NUTSHELL.
AND WHERE EXACTLY IS THIS HIDEAWAY?
"IT'S...IN AN ABANDONED U.S. MILITARY BASE BUILT INTO THE SIDE OF A CLIFF."
PROPERTY OF U.S. ARMY NO ADMITTANCE
"AND WHAT'S THE SECURITY LIKE? IT'S NOT UNPROTECTED, I ASSUME?"
"WELL...NO. WE BELIEVE VAN HORST HAS A NUMBER OF SOLDIERS-OF-FORTUNE IN HIS EMPLOY. PLUS, ONE OR MORE OF HIS LIEUTENANTS MAY BE ON-SITE."

GO ON TO THE NEXT PAGE.

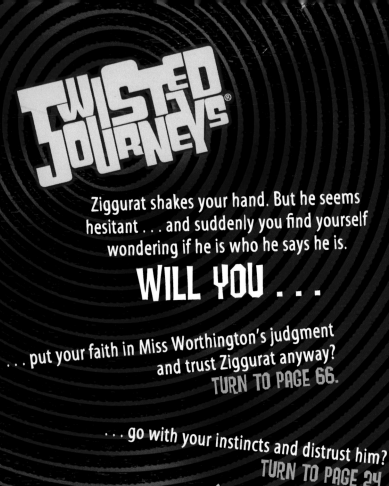

Ziggurat shakes your hand. But he seems hesitant . . . and suddenly you find yourself wondering if he is who he says he is.

WILL YOU . . .

. . . put your faith in Miss Worthington's judgment and trust Ziggurat anyway?
TURN TO PAGE 66.

. . . go with your instincts and distrust him?
TURN TO PAGE 24.

You know you and Eva are no match for Dolph and Wing together. The two of you turn on your heels and dash back the way you came . . .

. . . but your foot comes down hard on one particular section of the ancient stone flooring, and the entire floor collapses.

You and Eva fall with it, tumbling into a huge sub-subbasement chamber. As the stone floor rushes up to meet you in a bone-splintering impact, you can't help but think, *Wow, I really should have insisted that we block off that tunnel.*

THE END

You punch the first button, and the fire pictogram glows a brilliant red . . .

. . . and suddenly you're standing on a catwalk in what looks like an iron-melting plant of some kind.

You're inside an enormous building, and everywhere you look, automated machinery pours huge vats of molten metal into molds. And it's *hot!* You feel as if you've just stepped into an oven!

What could Van Horst want with this place? you wonder. You figure you'd better find your way outside or at least away from all this heat. You make your way along the catwalk, descend a short flight of stairs, and step out onto the concrete floor of the plant.

And there, standing not thirty feet away, is Franklin da Silva, Van Horst's super-deadly martial artist. You're caught right out in the open too— there's no cover anywhere.

Which is too bad, since da Silva spots you immediately.

GO ON TO THE NEXT PAGE.

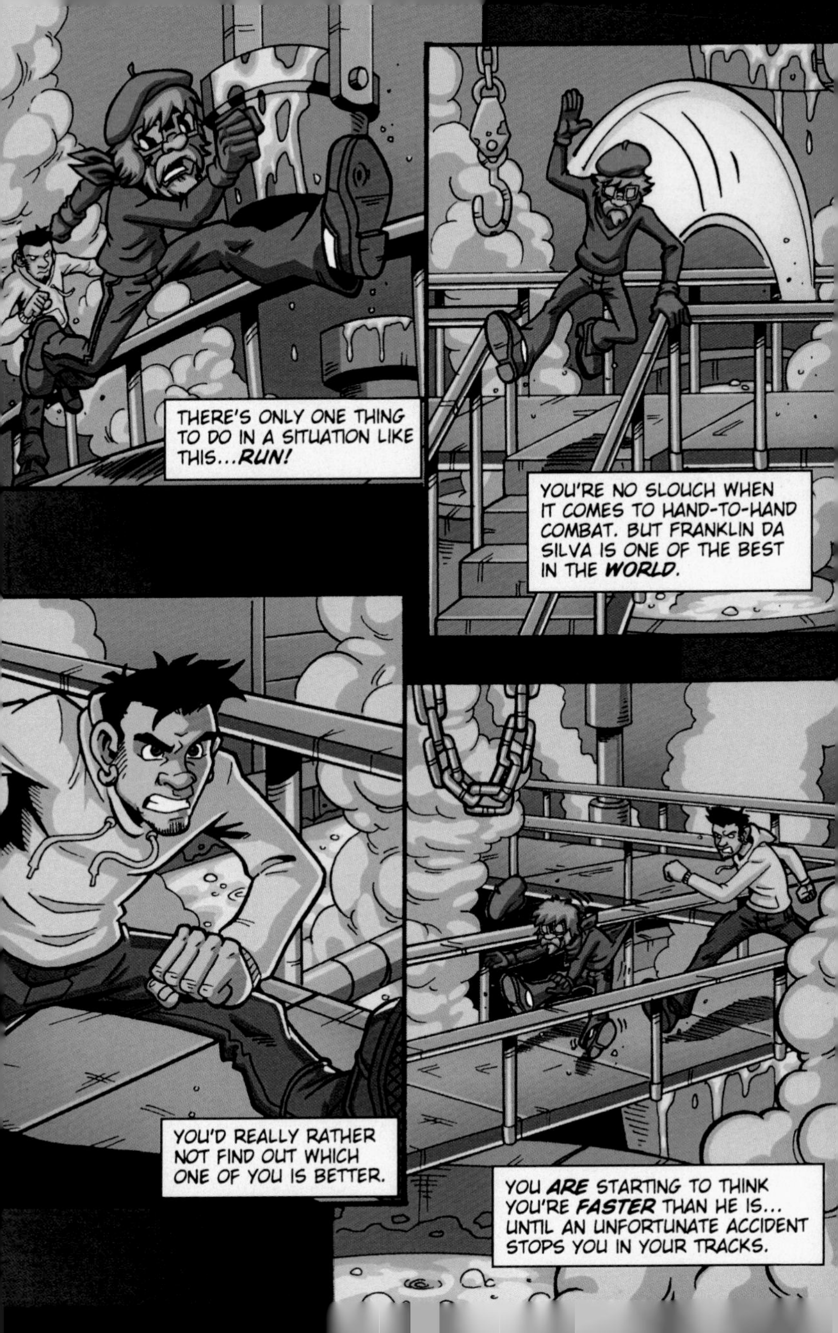
THERE'S ONLY ONE THING TO DO IN A SITUATION LIKE THIS...RUN!
YOU'RE NO SLOUCH WHEN IT COMES TO HAND-TO-HAND COMBAT. BUT FRANKLIN DA SILVA IS ONE OF THE BEST IN THE WORLD.
YOU'D REALLY RATHER NOT FIND OUT WHICH ONE OF YOU IS BETTER.
YOU ARE STARTING TO THINK YOU'RE FASTER THAN HE IS... UNTIL AN UNFORTUNATE ACCIDENT STOPS YOU IN YOUR TRACKS.

Your lead has disappeared—now he's
almost on top of you!

WILL YOU . . .

. . . dash across the bridge and still try to escape?

TURN TO PAGE 32.

. . . fight him and see if you can land a lucky shot?

TURN TO PAGE 41.

. . . offer him money to switch sides, since a
mercenary works for pay, after all?

TURN TO PAGE 59.

Slowly, carefully, you approach Martinique Stone. She lifts her head when you get close and looks at you with frightened eyes. "Oh, thank goodness, someone heard me!" she says. "Wing found out I was going to go over to the other side and tied me up. He was going to kill me!"

Stone is so grateful to you for untying her that she takes you straight to the EMP blaster, down deep in the catacombs. You and Dolph and Eva use a high-frequency scan-corder to analyze the equipment and beam all the information back to Miss Worthington. Then you set explosives around it and blow the whole thing to bits.

Miss Worthington is very pleased with your performance—so much so, in fact, that she sends you on an all-expenses-paid vacation to the destination of your choice.

Tropical beaches, here you come!

THE END

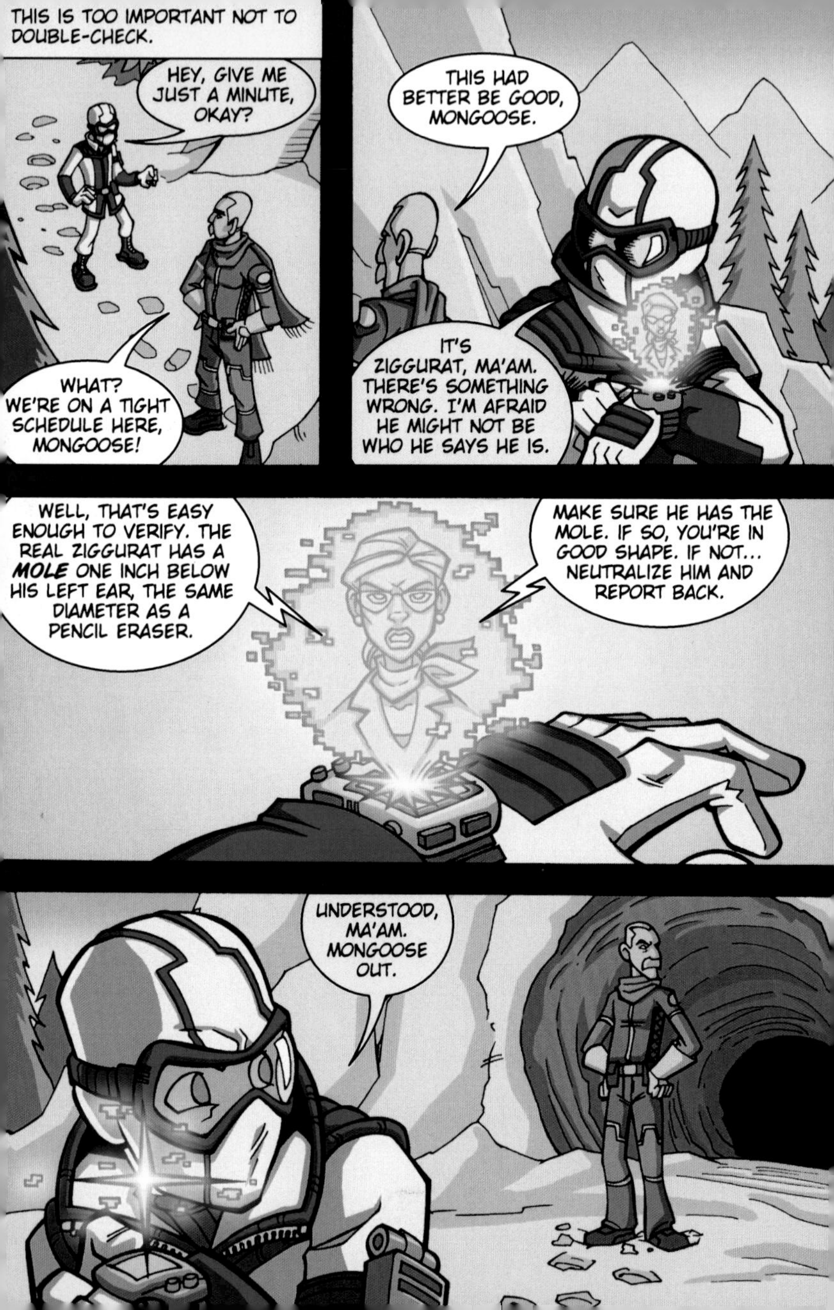
THIS IS TOO IMPORTANT NOT TO DOUBLE-CHECK.
HEY, GIVE ME JUST A MINUTE, OKAY?
WHAT? WE'RE ON A TIGHT SCHEDULE HERE, MONGOOSE!
THIS HAD BETTER BE GOOD, MONGOOSE.
IT'S ZIGGURAT, MA'AM. THERE'S SOMETHING WRONG. I'M AFRAID HE MIGHT NOT BE WHO HE SAYS HE IS.
WELL, THAT'S EASY ENOUGH TO VERIFY. THE REAL ZIGGURAT HAS A ***MOLE*** ONE INCH BELOW HIS LEFT EAR, THE SAME DIAMETER AS A PENCIL ERASER.
MAKE SURE HE HAS THE MOLE. IF SO, YOU'RE IN GOOD SHAPE. IF NOT... NEUTRALIZE HIM AND REPORT BACK.
UNDERSTOOD, MA'AM. MONGOOSE OUT.

A mole on his neck, huh? Well, that should be easy enough to verify.

You move up closer to Ziggurat—and you realize that he's wearing a heavy wool scarf, wrapped around his neck several times. There's no way to see the mole with that scarf there!

You think quickly as the two of you move through the ice tunnel. If he *is* the real Code name: Ziggurat, then you have nothing to worry about. But if he's *not* . . . then your life is in extreme danger and he could kill you at any moment.

"That's a nice scarf," you tell him. "What's it made of?"

He frowns, confused. "My scarf? I don't know. It's a scarf."

You keep going. "May I look at it? I'd like to buy one like it."

"My sister made this scarf." He points ahead. "Come on, it's this way."

GO ON TO THE NEXT PAGE.

Ziggurat dashes ahead. You have no choice but to follow him. Your heart beats hard and fast—you've got to stay on your guard, against Ziggurat *and* everything else around here.

Soon the tunnel ends at a grate set in the ceiling. Ziggurat moves the grate aside and sticks his head up through it. Then he motions for you to follow as he scrambles up through the opening. "Come on!"

You emerge into a place that looks like a huge, abandoned auto garage. You realize this was the motor pool for the base. But it's hard to think about where you are, because you're constantly keeping an eye on Ziggurat. What if he turns on you?

Then you spot an opportunity! His scarf has come loose. You still can't see his neck, but you think you could just reach out and yank the scarf right off him.

GO ON TO THE NEXT PAGE.

It all comes down to trust. Ziggurat knew where to meet you, at the secret airstrip, so he's probably who he says he is. But what if Van Horst got to him somehow?

WILL YOU . . .

. . . pull the scarf off, just to be absolutely sure?
TURN TO PAGE 62.

. . . keep cooperating with him, since he's done nothing wrong so far?
TURN TO PAGE 46.

You don't know how long it'll be before Van Horst shows himself, or sends someone or something after you. But you figure you'd better take a good look around the place while you have the chance.

It only takes a minute for you to locate the EMP blaster—and the hypno-beam is here too! *Jackpot!* On top of those, you find three other devices that you can't readily identify. One of them has a lot of meteorology symbols on it. Is Van Horst also trying to control the weather?

Then your head snaps around as you hear a deep voice over at one side of the room. Two figures have appeared in the shadows there—they must have come through some hidden hatch.

"So this is Code name: Mongoose," Van Horst says, stepping into the light. You squint to see who is with him . . .

GO ON TO THE NEXT PAGE.

PERHAPS YOU KNOW MY NEW FRIEND AND COLLEAGUE?

THERE'S *NO WAY*. NO WAY! YOU CAN'T *BELIEVE* IT, BUT STANDING THERE NEXT TO VAN HORST IS...

...*MISS WORTHINGTON!*

GO ON TO THE NEXT PAGE.

WILL YOU . . .

. . . accept that your boss has betrayed you and try to take them both out?
TURN TO PAGE 75.

. . . trust Miss Worthington and try to work with her to defeat Van Horst?
TURN TO PAGE 105.

"Get inside, everyone!" you tell them. "I'll hold them off!"

"And how are you going to do that, Mongoose?" Van Horst demands. "Scold my men for misbehaving?"

You climb up into the escape pod. "No," you shout to Van Horst. "But I think I will rewire this control panel so the dome floods once we launch."

You're just close enough to see Van Horst's face go pale. "No, Mongoose! Don't! Men, stop!"

Your bluff worked! The mercenaries back off, and your escape craft drifts up and away from the undersea dome. You're safe!

One of the scientists says, "You look sad, Mongoose. What's wrong?"

You shrug. "We didn't get him. I mean, I'm glad you guys are okay, but Van Horst is still loose."

"Don't worry, kid," the man says. "Now that we're safe, we can undo every single thing Van Horst is trying to do."

Maybe that's good enough.

THE END

You have to try to make one last dash for it. Your feet barely touch the metal of the bridge as you sprint across it and slam through the door on the other side.

You find yourself in the middle of a hallway. To your left, through a doorway, you see a room filled with high-tech equipment—including the electromagnetic-pulse blaster! To your right, there's a door with a beautiful red EXIT sign glowing above it.

You could try to destroy the EMP blaster, but da Silva is right behind you, and if he catches you, you're pretty sure it's all over.

Or you could escape to the outside and maybe not get mangled, but that leaves the EMP blaster untouched.

You can hear da Silva's footsteps on the other side of the door, getting closer in a hurry.

GO ON TO THE NEXT PAGE.

This is a tough choice,
and you've got to make it quickly.

WILL YOU . . .

. . . try to take out the EMP blaster?
TURN TO PAGE 45.

. . . make a run for the door
and then figure out how to
complete your assignment?
TURN TO PAGE 69.

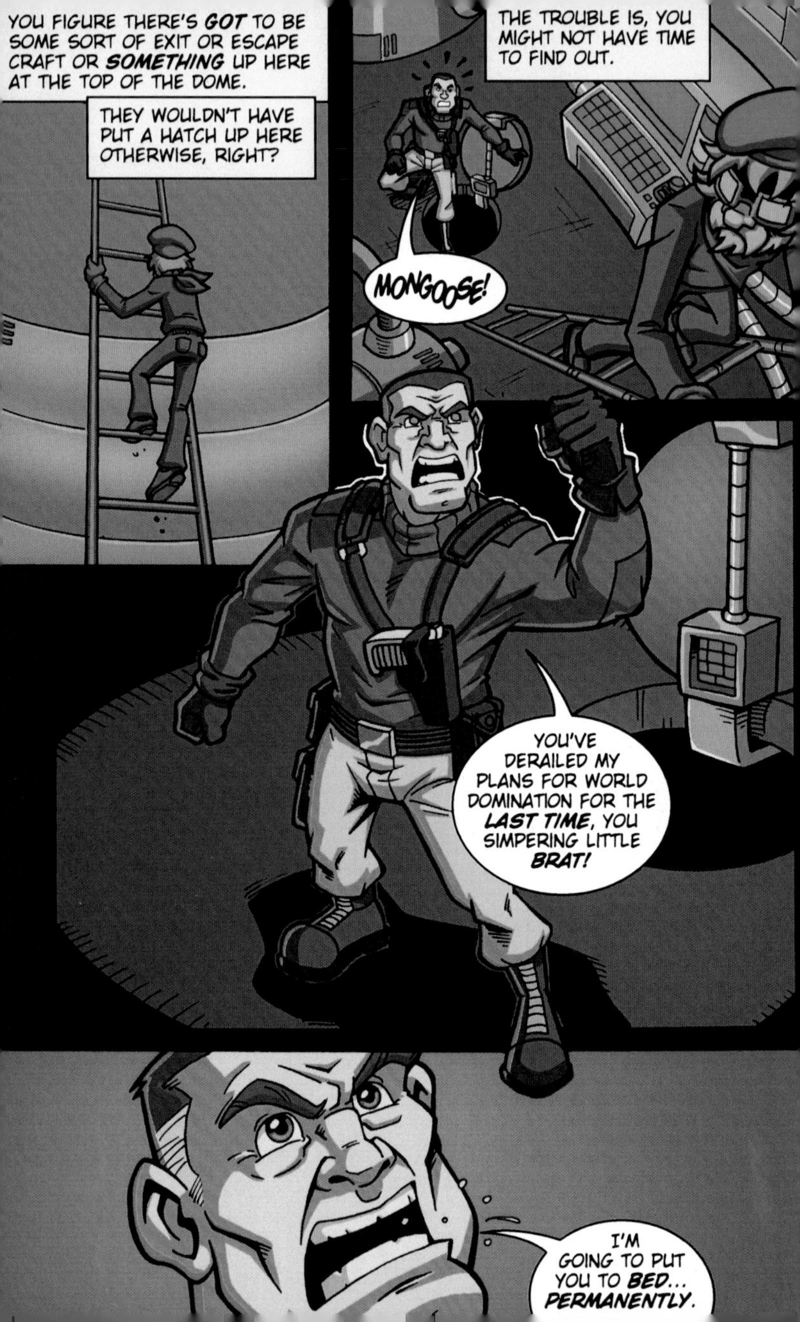
YOU FIGURE THERE'S GOT TO BE SOME SORT OF EXIT OR ESCAPE CRAFT OR SOMETHING UP HERE AT THE TOP OF THE DOME.
THEY WOULDN'T HAVE PUT A HATCH UP HERE OTHERWISE, RIGHT?
THE TROUBLE IS, YOU MIGHT NOT HAVE TIME TO FIND OUT.
MONGOOSE!
YOU'VE DERAILED MY PLANS FOR WORLD DOMINATION FOR THE LAST TIME, YOU SIMPERING LITTLE BRAT!
I'M GOING TO PUT YOU TO BED... PERMANENTLY.

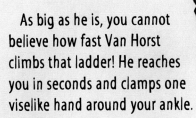

As big as he is, you cannot believe how fast Van Horst climbs that ladder! He reaches you in seconds and clamps one viselike hand around your ankle.

"Might as well give up now, Mongoose!" he snarls. With his free hand, he pops open a pouch at his belt, and three tiny, whirring robots, like little helicopters, come flying out— and then they start shooting laser beams at you!

You flip around and duck as best you can, but you get tagged a couple of times. Those things *hurt!*

"Even if you can get away from me," Van Horst shouts, "you'll never get away from my wing-stings!"

A laser beam scorches your arm, and you start to think Van Horst might be right!

TURN TO PAGE 88.

"Just a minute, Ziggurat!" you say. "How do I know I can trust you?"

He turns. "What?"

"I saw that knife! You're working for Van Horst, aren't you?"

Ziggurat's face gets very angry. "The *outrage!*" he bellows. "I will not stand for this! This assignment is *over* for you!"

It's not long before you're back in Miss Worthington's office. As it turns out, Ziggurat is one of her most trusted agents . . . and the knife you saw was a trophy from an earlier mission. "You've disappointed me, Mongoose," Miss Worthington says grimly. "This kind of poor judgment cannot go unanswered. I'm pulling you off this assignment . . . and giving it to Code name: Topaz."

You leave Miss Worthington's office with your head hanging low. "I guess next time I'll be less suspicious," you grumble.

Topaz is *never* going to let you hear the end of this.

THE END

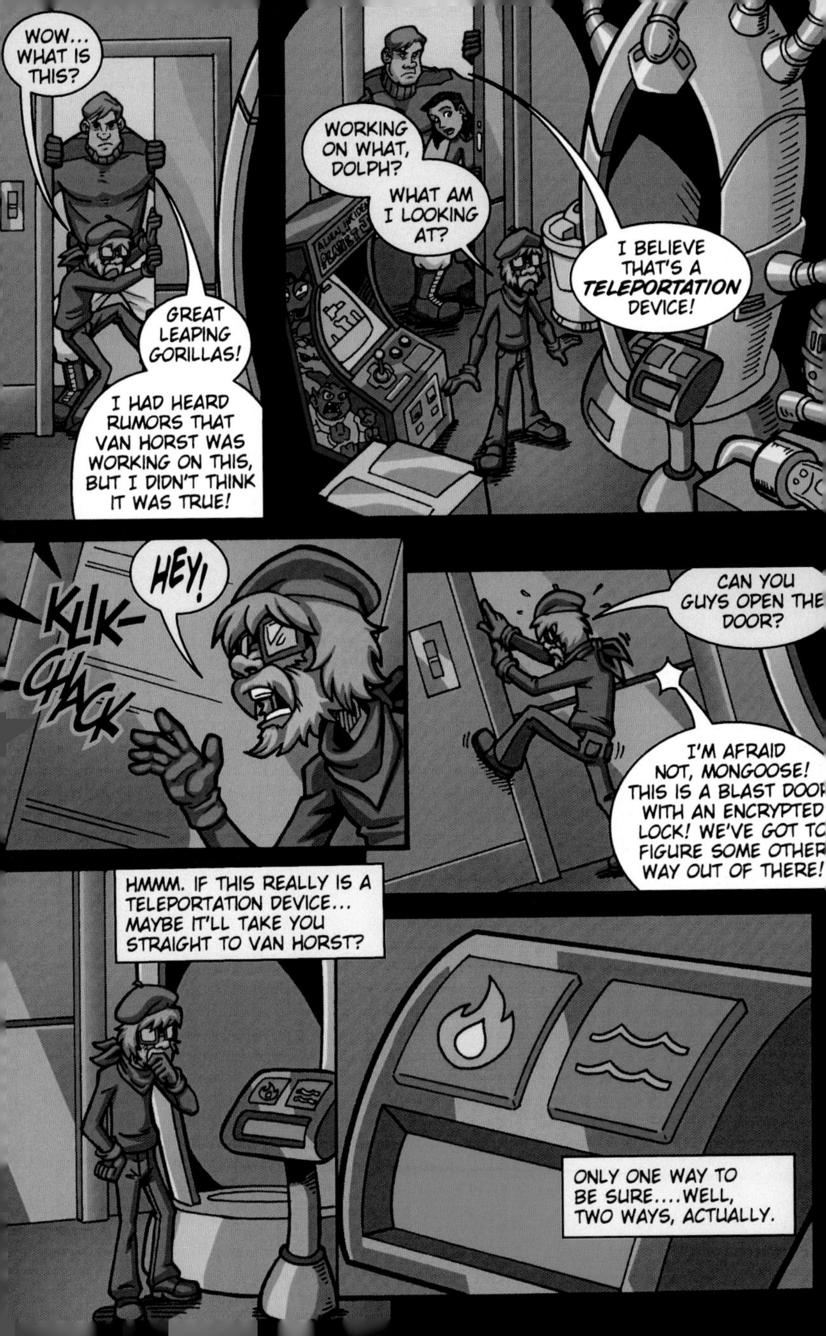
WOW... WHAT IS THIS?
GREAT LEAPING GORILLAS!
I HAD HEARD RUMORS THAT VAN HORST WAS WORKING ON THIS, BUT I DIDN'T THINK IT WAS TRUE!
WORKING ON WHAT, DOLPH?
WHAT AM I LOOKING AT?
I BELIEVE THAT'S A **TELEPORTATION** DEVICE!
KLIK-CHACK
HEY!
CAN YOU GUYS OPEN THE DOOR?
I'M AFRAID NOT, MONGOOSE! THIS IS A BLAST DOOR WITH AN ENCRYPTED LOCK! WE'VE GOT TO FIGURE SOME OTHER WAY OUT OF THERE!
HMMM. IF THIS REALLY IS A TELEPORTATION DEVICE... MAYBE IT'LL TAKE YOU STRAIGHT TO VAN HORST?
ONLY ONE WAY TO BE SURE....WELL, TWO WAYS, ACTUALLY.

You're pretty sure you're not getting out of here unless you press one of those buttons.

WILL YOU . . .

. . . try the button with the "fire" symbol?
TURN TO PAGE 20.

. . . take a chance with the other button and the "water" symbol?
TURN TO PAGE 10

These creatures are everywhere! But if you can get back to the stairs, you can call in reinforcements. Moving as fast as you can, you bend down and grab a flash bomb out of a secret compartment in your shoe. These creatures don't look as if they see much light. Maybe you can blind them and get away!

You throw the flash bomb and turn your head, and even with your eyes closed, you can see the glare as it goes off. Okay! Time to sprint!

But even as you start running, slimy hands reach out and grab you. The flash didn't affect them in the tiniest bit. With a sinking feeling in your stomach, you realize these monstrosities are actually *blind*. They didn't see the light at *all*.

But *you* see, as they drag you and Dolph back into their horrible, muck-filled dens, that this is definitely . . .

THE END

You're pretty sure you and Eva could take Dolph . . . or Wing . . . but the two of them together? You just don't know!

WILL YOU . . .

. . . try to run for it and hope you can make it to safety?
TURN TO PAGE 19.

. . . stand with Eva and fight Dolph and Wing both?
TURN TO PAGE 53.

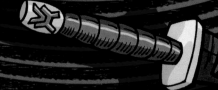

You recognize the fighting style that Franklin da Silva is using. It's a mixture of Muay Thai and Tae Kwon Do . . . but you're skilled in both of those disciplines. Plus you've spent years studying Snow Tiger Kung Fu. Maybe . . . *maybe* you can take him.

Da Silva comes in with a flurry of aerial kicks, but you counter those with some well-aimed punches to the ribs. He jabs a fist straight at your nose, but you block him and sweep his feet out from under him. The fight goes back and forth, but you're holding your own!

That is, until you remember that he's a bad guy . . . and he fights *really* dirty. You feel a sting in your ankle and look down to see that he's injected you with a tiny needle sticking out of his ring. Immediately, the paralyzing poison starts to work.

"Sorry, Mongoose," he says. "Lights out for you."

THE END

As soon as you arrive in Paris—at one of the Agency's private airfields—your two contacts meet you. One is a tall, muscular man with thick, red hair. The other is a slender woman with dark hair and brilliant green eyes. They introduce themselves as Dolph and Eva.

"Those aren't your real names, are they?" you ask.

"Of course not, child," Eva replies. "No more than your real name is Mongoose."

"Come on," Dolph rumbles. "We have to get you disguised."

You *hate* wearing disguises, even though you're very good at it. "Do I have to?"

Eva nods impatiently. "We can't have a child running around the streets of Paris unsupervised, now can we?"

Soon, with makeup and a wig, they turn you into . . . a little old Frenchman!

You sigh. "I guess this'll work."

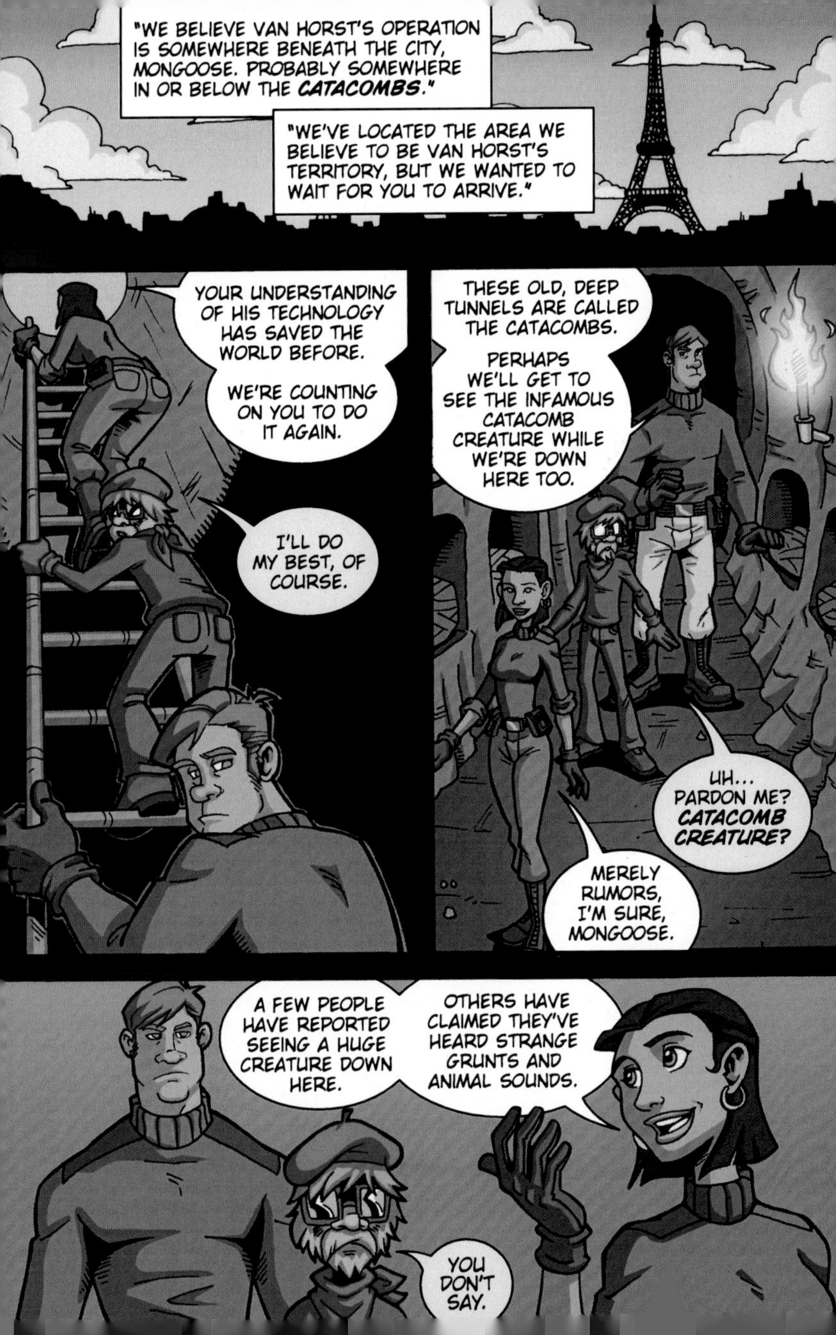
"WE BELIEVE VAN HORST'S OPERATION IS SOMEWHERE BENEATH THE CITY, MONGOOSE. PROBABLY SOMEWHERE IN OR BELOW THE CATACOMBS."
"WE'VE LOCATED THE AREA WE BELIEVE TO BE VAN HORST'S TERRITORY, BUT WE WANTED TO WAIT FOR YOU TO ARRIVE."
YOUR UNDERSTANDING OF HIS TECHNOLOGY HAS SAVED THE WORLD BEFORE.
WE'RE COUNTING ON YOU TO DO IT AGAIN.
I'LL DO MY BEST, OF COURSE.
THESE OLD, DEEP TUNNELS ARE CALLED THE CATACOMBS.
PERHAPS WE'LL GET TO SEE THE INFAMOUS CATACOMB CREATURE WHILE WE'RE DOWN HERE TOO.
UH... PARDON ME? CATACOMB CREATURE?
MERELY RUMORS, I'M SURE, MONGOOSE.
A FEW PEOPLE HAVE REPORTED SEEING A HUGE CREATURE DOWN HERE.
OTHERS HAVE CLAIMED THEY'VE HEARD STRANGE GRUNTS AND ANIMAL SOUNDS.
YOU DON'T SAY.

TWISTED JOURNEYS®

You know the EMP blaster is what you're supposed to be going after. But no one mentioned a monster before!

WILL YOU . . .

. . . take a side trip and investigate this mysterious Catacomb Creature?
TURN TO PAGE 83.

. . . stick to the plan and go after the EMP blaster?
TURN TO PAGE 106.

You can't just run away. So you streak toward the room with the EMP blaster—and da Silva bursts through the door behind you, hot on your heels.

"I'll get you, Mongoose!" he shouts. "I'll make you sorry you were ever born!"

Wait—you've got an idea! "If I have to listen to you talk anymore, da Silva, I *will* be sorry I was ever born!" you shout. Da Silva roars and puts on an extra burst of speed . . .

. . . and as you get into the room with the EMP blaster, da Silva launches a flying kick, aimed straight at your head. But you fling yourself flat to the floor . . .

. . . and da Silva's kick crashes straight through the EMP blaster. There's a huge flare of electricity, and for da Silva *and* the device, that's all she wrote.

Time to pack it up and head home. Score one for the good guys!

THE END

YOU FIGURE YOU'RE PROBABLY JUST BEING PARANOID. IT'D BE BEST TO CONCENTRATE ON GETTING YOUR ASSIGNMENT DONE, AS FAST AS POSSIBLE.

WOW... THIS PLACE IS *HUGE*...

IT'S BIG, YES. BUT WE ONLY NEED TO WORRY ABOUT THAT BUILDING WITH THE SATELLITE DISHES ON TOP. THAT'S OUR OBJECTIVE.

GO ON TO THE NEXT PAGE.

"Here's the breakdown," Ziggurat whispers, as the two of you hide behind a big stack of crates. "I think what we're after is inside that building right in the middle of the whole place. We've got to get in there—"

You break in. "And blow it up?"

He looks impatient. "Not just blow it up! We have to understand what Van Horst is doing. We need *you* to analyze the equipment, take lots of pictures . . . and *then* we can blow it up."

You start to move in, but he puts his hand on your arm and stops you. "Also, I don't want you to hurt anybody."

"Huh? What do you mean?"

"Our fight is with Van Horst, not with his henchmen. So don't hurt anybody, plain and simple. Okay?"

You nod your head, confused.

GO ON TO THE NEXT PAGE.

Now you're *really* suspicious. It's not that you were planning to do anybody any harm—your mission focuses on the equipment Van Horst is using. But all these armed guards are working for Van Horst, and you're pretty sure they wouldn't hesitate to turn *you* into a piece of swiss cheese.

Why would Ziggurat ask you not to hurt any of them? Unless . . . he *is* working for the other side?

You've seen plenty of strange things over the course of your career as a secret agent. People who've been kidnapped have turned around and sided with their kidnappers. Operatives who were supposed to be perfectly loyal have sold national secrets to spies from other countries. Maybe something like that has happened with Ziggurat.

Or worse yet . . . maybe someone is *forcing* him to side with the enemy.

And it's still possible that this guy isn't even Ziggurat at all.

GO ON TO THE NEXT PAGE.

If you're going to do something, it had better be right now and it had better be decisive. Otherwise, you might as well trust Ziggurat and forget about your suspicions.

WILL YOU . . .

. . . pull your gun on Ziggurat and force him to take off the neck scarf?
TURN TO PAGE 70.

. . . forget your fears and help him get inside the central building?
TURN TO PAGE 90.

"I think I've got to go with downstairs," you say. "I don't trust that staircase too much, and down should be safer than up."

Eva smiles sweetly at you while Dolph sulks. "Mongoose shows good judgment," she says.

When Dolph speaks, his words come out pretty surly. "All right, fine. Overrule me. You two lead the way then. Go on, go!"

Eva takes the lead, and the three of you begin to descend into the lower regions of the cathedral. Soon you emerge into an area very similar to the catacombs you came through to get here—a damp, dark series of tunnels and caverns.

"Wow," you breathe out. "Van Horst could be hiding *anything* down here!"

And it's just then that you hear a strange, wet, slithering noise from behind you.

And in front of you.

And off to both sides.

GO ON TO THE NEXT PAGE.

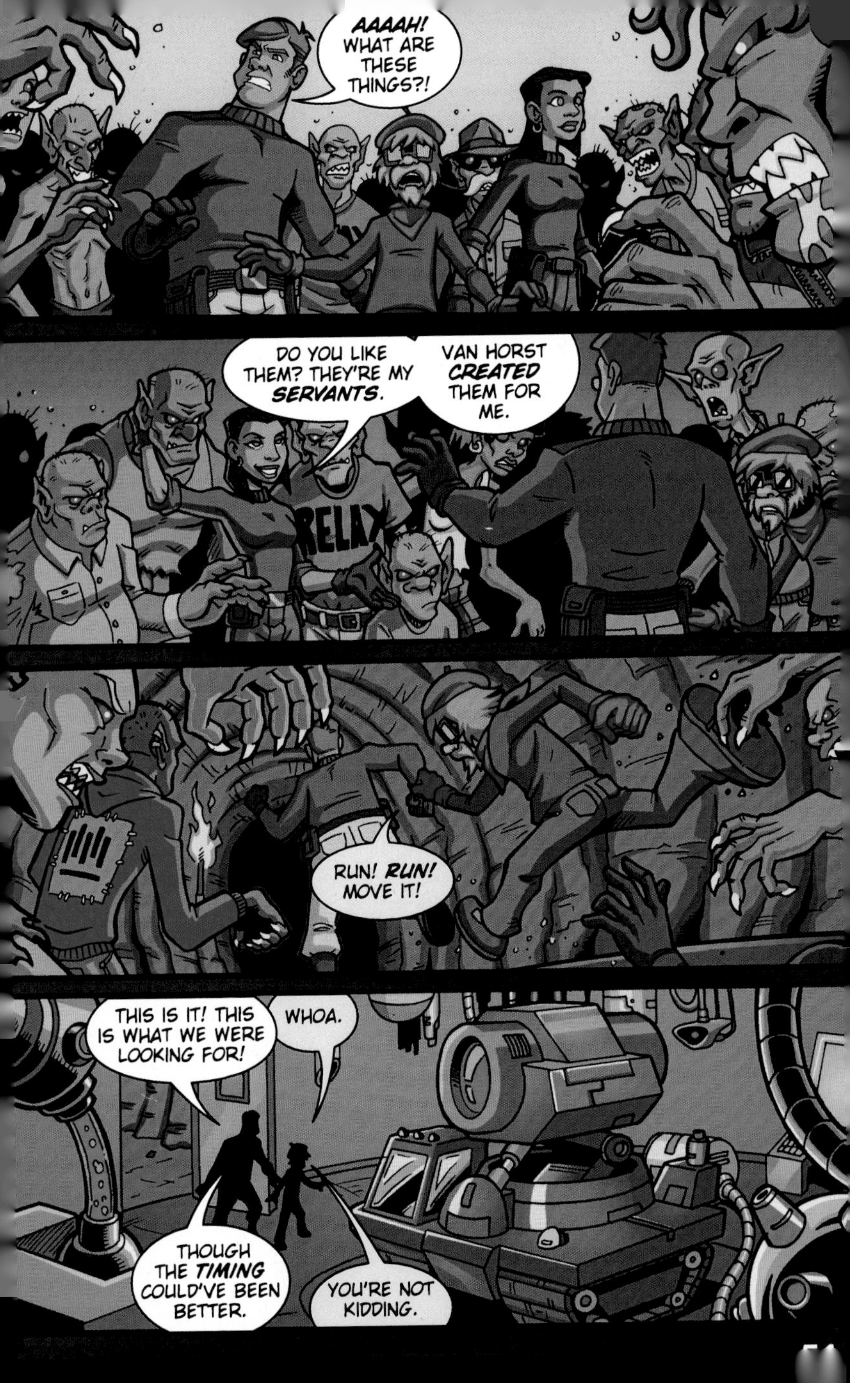
AAAAH! WHAT ARE THESE THINGS?!
DO YOU LIKE THEM? THEY'RE MY SERVANTS.
VAN HORST CREATED THEM FOR ME.
RELAX
RUN! RUN! MOVE IT!
THIS IS IT! THIS IS WHAT WE WERE LOOKING FOR!
WHOA.
THOUGH THE TIMING COULD'VE BEEN BETTER.
YOU'RE NOT KIDDING.

You're in an awfully tight spot!

WILL YOU . . .

. . . create a diversion and try to escape?
TURN TO PAGE 39.

. . . try to convince these creatures that
you and Dolph are the good guys?
TURN TO PAGE 60.

You and Eva plant your feet and get ready to fight as Dolph and Wing get closer.

Or at least, you want them to *think* you're getting ready to fight.

As soon as they get within a certain distance, you pop loose three tiny pellets from a secret compartment inside your wristwatch and hurl them to the floor. Clouds of knockout gas billow up and surround everyone. Within seconds everyone's asleep except you. You've built up an immunity to this particular gas.

After Dolph and Wing are tied up, it's no trouble finding the room with the EMP blaster in it. But you also find a radio transmitter . . . and you recognize Van Horst's voice coming through it!

"What's going on there?" he demands.

"This is Code name: Mongoose," you murmur into the microphone. "I didn't get you today, Van Horst. But I'm coming for you. *Soon.*"

THE END

"That's Martinique Stone!" you whisper to Ziggurat. "*The* Martinique Stone! Do you know how *dangerous* she is? Let's neutralize her, *then* go after all the hypno-beam equipment."

Ziggurat hesitates. "But we're supposed to eliminate the hypno-beam *first*. That's our prime objective."

You wave away his concerns with one hand. "We'll get to that. Besides, what if she walked in on us right in the middle of planting all the explosives? She could ruin everything!"

"All right," he says, after a moment. "Let's go."

GO ON TO THE NEXT PAGE.

THIS COULDN'T BE ANY BETTER. STONE HAS NO IDEA YOU'RE THERE, SO YOU CAN SNEAK UP ON HER WITHOUT ANY TROUBLE.

AT LEAST, THAT'S THE PLAN...

WAIT, WAIT, STOP! STOP!

HUH? WHAT'S WRONG?

IT'S MARTINIQUE...

I CAN'T LET YOU HURT HER! I KNOW SHE'S WORKING FOR THE WRONG SIDE, BUT...

...I'M IN LOVE WITH HER! WE'VE BEEN SEEING EACH OTHER IN SECRET FOR THE LAST YEAR!

GO ON TO THE NEXT PAGE.

Getting friendly with the enemy is treason!
But if he can convince her to switch sides,
she could be incredibly valuable.

WILL YOU . . .

. . . try to overpower Ziggurat and turn
him in to Miss Worthington?
TURN TO PAGE 101.

. . . convince Ziggurat to
turn himself in peacefully?
TURN TO PAGE 85.

. . . try to get Ziggurat to convince Martinique
Stone to defect to your side?
TURN TO PAGE 80.

. . . overpower both of them,
since then you'd be a hero?
TURN TO PAGE 74.

The three of you rush into the room, confident you can overpower Wing together.

Except . . .

"Ha *ha!*" Wing laughs. "Fresh toys to play with!"

From the first punch, you realize Wing really *is* a monster. He's stronger than anyone you've ever seen and fast as a cat. He slams Dolph and Eva into a wall and then turns to come for you . . .

. . . but he should've been more careful. Dolph's impact knocked loose a couple of rocks in the ceiling, and you can see *just* where one is about to fall.

"Lights out, kid!" Wing shouts.

You sweep his legs so that he falls directly into the path of the plummeting rock. Turns out it's lights out for *him*. And with Wing out of the picture, destroying the EMP blaster will be a snap.

You can accomplish your mission and even take your time doing it.

Life is good.

THE END

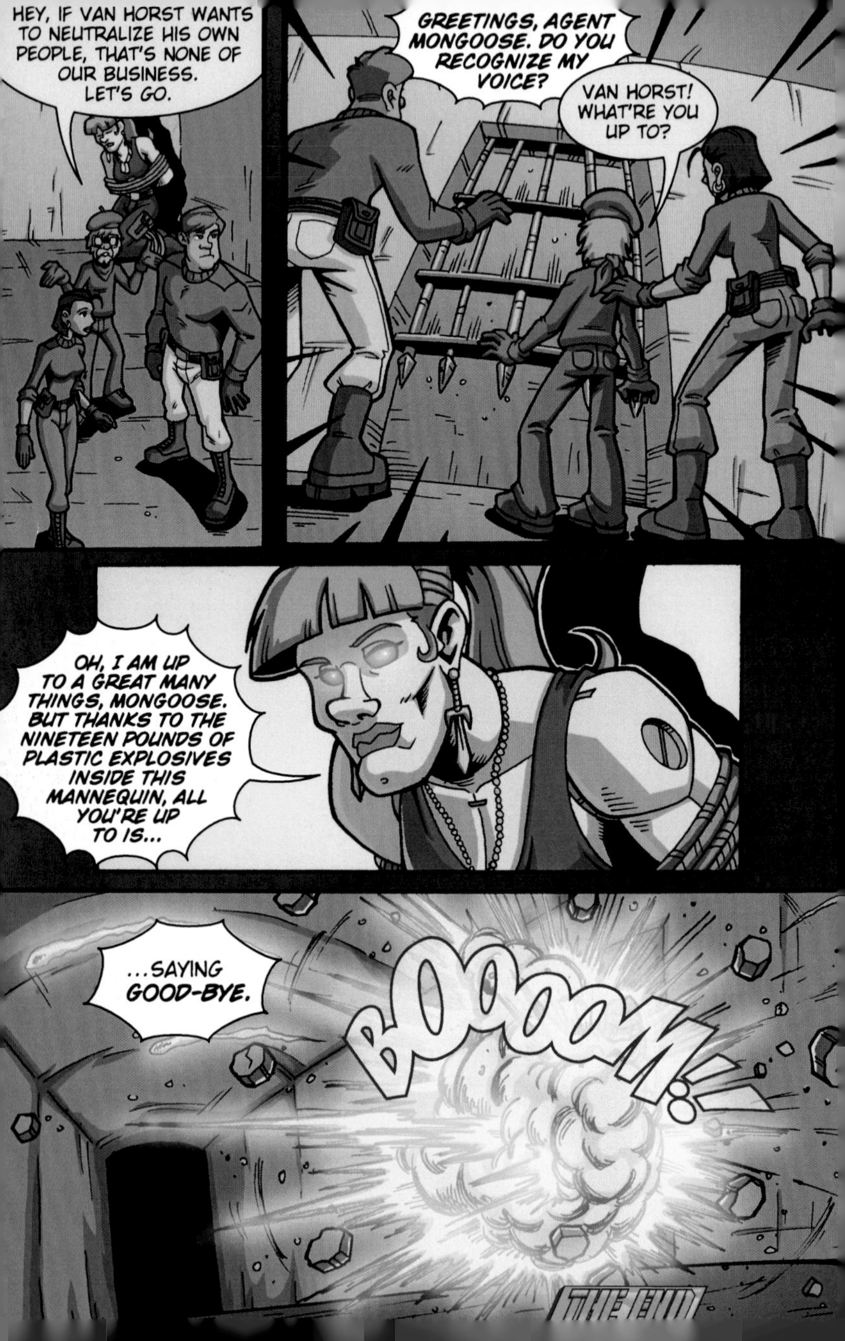
HEY, IF VAN HORST WANTS TO NEUTRALIZE HIS OWN PEOPLE, THAT'S NONE OF OUR BUSINESS. LET'S GO.
GREETINGS, AGENT MONGOOSE. DO YOU RECOGNIZE MY VOICE?
VAN HORST! WHAT'RE YOU UP TO?
OH, I AM UP TO A GREAT MANY THINGS, MONGOOSE. BUT THANKS TO THE NINETEEN POUNDS OF PLASTIC EXPLOSIVES INSIDE THIS MANNEQUIN, ALL YOU'RE UP TO IS...
...SAYING GOOD-BYE.
BOOOOM!!
THE END

You spin around and hold out your hands. "Wait, hang on, just wait a minute!" you shout to da Silva. "Listen to me!"

He pauses just as he's about to set foot on the bridge and eyes you warily. "What?"

"Look, you're a mercenary, right?"

Da Silva puffs up his chest. "I'm a private security contractor."

You wave your hand impatiently. "I don't have time to go running around like this. I'll pay you twice what Van Horst is paying you. What do you say?"

Da Silva considers this for a moment.

Then he pulls a small black box out of a jacket pocket and slaps it onto the metal bridge railing. "I say, you have a lot to learn about loyalty." Da Silva hits a switch on the box, and as the bridge crackles with deadly electricity, it becomes clear that you made a *truly* poor choice in trying to bribe him.

THE END

"Wait! Wait! Stop!" you shout. They *don't* stop—but it occurs to you that you're in Paris, so you switch to French and say the same thing.

That gets through to them! They pause, and then one of them answers you, also in French. "Stop? Why should we?"

"Because I'm not the bad guy here!" You point at Eva. "*She* is! She works for a horrible, evil man named Van Horst. You don't have to do what she says! She's just using you. If you agree not to hurt me or my friend Dolph, I can help you!"

"Don't listen to the child, you idiotic *brutes*!" Eva screams. "Only listen to *me*! I know what's best for you!"

The creature who spoke earlier takes a step forward and sniffs the air near you. "If we help you," he asks, "what's in it for us?"

GO ON TO THE NEXT PAGE.

These creatures . . . these *people* . . . are the weirdest things you've ever seen, but that doesn't mean they're evil. You just have to handle this situation properly.

WILL YOU . . .

. . . promise them a lot of money from Miss Worthington if they help you?
TURN TO PAGE 86.

. . . explain to them that if they help you, they can learn to have better lives than this?
TURN TO PAGE 81.

ALMOST THERE... *ALMOST THERE...*

HEY-- *HEY! QUIT IT!*

HAVE YOU GONE *INSANE?*

YOU BREATHE A *HUGE* SIGH OF RELIEF WHEN YOU SEE THE EXACT MOLE MISS WORTHINGTON DESCRIBED.

THIS IS CODE NAME: ZIGGURAT, NO QUESTION ABOUT IT.

I HAD TO BE SURE YOU WERE WHO YOU SAID YOU WERE. I CALLED MISS WORTHINGTON, AND SHE TOLD ME ABOUT THE MOLE ON YOUR NECK.

SO YOU SUSPECTED I WAS ONE OF VAN HORST'S PEOPLE? UGH! I'VE NEVER BEEN SO OUTRAGED IN MY ENTIRE LIFE!

YEAH, WELL, CAN WE JUST GET ON WITH IT NOW? WE HAVE SOME EXPLOSIVES TO SET, DON'T WE?

GO ON TO THE NEXT PAGE.

The rest of the operation goes as smoothly as clockwork.

Your reputation as an expert in electronics and explosives is well deserved. You and Ziggurat sneak into the old army base, bypass the guards *and* the security system, and plant enough explosives to blow the whole place to tiny bits. You even alert the personnel inside before the bombs go off, so they can all evacuate.

But as you and your colleague speed away on your snowmobiles from the site of the explosion, there's still tension in the air between the two of you. Ziggurat hasn't forgiven you for not trusting him. You're not certain he ever will.

And you *hate* having bad blood like this between agents.

GO ON TO THE NEXT PAGE.

You've seriously offended your partner on this mission. But weren't you right to be suspicious?

WILL YOU . . .

. . . keep quiet and hope the whole mistrust incident blows over?
TURN TO PAGE 98.

. . . confront Ziggurat—again—because it's best to be doubly sure?
TURN TO PAGE 82.

You lead the way as the three of you start climbing the stairs. "Are you sure about this?" Eva asks.

"No," you reply. "But we have to be thorough, right?"

She nods—but as soon as Dolph gets on the stairs, his weight starts making them tremble and shake. "Bad idea!" you shout. "It's not safe! Everybody down!"

But it's too late. The staircase buckles and collapses, and you and Eva and Dolph are all caught in an avalanche of ancient wood and metal.

You wake up in the hospital. Miss Worthington is standing there, waiting for you to regain consciousness . . . and you think she might say something like, "Oh, thank goodness, you're still alive!"

But instead, she says, "That was one seriously bungled mission, Mongoose. We're lucky Code name: Topaz was in the area to pick up the pieces. Once you've recovered . . . consider yourself suspended."

THE END

You grin at your fellow agent, though it's hidden behind your thermal mask. "Okay, partner," you tell him. "Lead the way."

Ziggurat nods and takes you outside to a pair of snowmobiles. You trail him out into the wilderness for what seems like hours. Finally, he stops on the slope of a hill, shuts off his snowmobile, and motions for you to follow him.

The two of you creep up the hill and peer over to the other side. Below, in a small valley, you see the entrance of what appears to be an ice cave. "It's a secret back door," Ziggurat explains. "We can get almost the whole way inside using this."

With Ziggurat leading the way, the two of you sneak down the hill and enter the ice cave.

GO ON TO THE NEXT PAGE.

SO FAR, SO GOOD. ZIGGURAT MOVES VERY QUIETLY. VERY PROFESSIONALLY.

THE THING IS...YOU'VE READ ZIGGURAT'S FILE. YOU KNOW HOW *DANGEROUS* HE IS.

YOU'RE THE TECHNICAL EXPERT ON THIS TRIP, AND CODE NAME: ZIGGURAT IS THE *MUSCLE*. IF HE TURNS AGAINST YOU...

...*WAIT* A MINUTE!

IS THAT WHAT YOU *THINK* IT IS?

THAT'S ONE OF VAN HORST'S KNIVES! ONE OF THE ONES HE HAD CUSTOM-MADE FOR HIS PRIVATE COLLECTION!

WHY DOES ZIGGURAT HAVE IT...?

GO ON TO THE NEXT PAGE.

That's one of Van Horst's knives, no question about it. Your suspicions of Ziggurat might have been right on the money. But can you be sure?

WILL YOU . . .

. . . surprise-attack Ziggurat and ask questions once he's no longer a threat?
TURN TO PAGE 79.

. . . confront him verbally and demand to know the truth about the knife?
TURN TO PAGE 36.

. . . keep playing along and see what else you can find out?
TURN TO PAGE 104.

You know destroying Van Horst's EMP blaster is important, but you can't do that if you're dead, can you? You spin to the right and beat feet toward the EXIT sign . . .

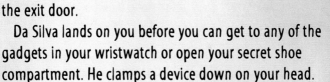

. . . but you hear the sound of a snare-trap gun being fired . . .

. . . and steel cables wrap around your ankles. You fall flat on your face, ten feet from the exit door.

Da Silva lands on you before you can get to any of the gadgets in your wristwatch or open your secret shoe compartment. He clamps a device down on your head.

"What's that?" you demand. "What're you doing to me?"

"This is a personality reverser," da Silva explains. "Once it's done with you, you'll be Van Horst's loyal new lackey."

No! Code name: Mongoose can't end like this!

But the device clicks on, and suddenly you realize . . . Van Horst was right all along!

It'll be *great* helping him take over the world!

THE END

"Hold it right there," you snap at Ziggurat. You've drawn your pistol and aimed it right at him. Your hand doesn't shake at all, and you let your voice get a little dangerous.

"What is this?" he demands, outraged. "You're one of Van Horst's people?"

You roll your eyes. "No! I work for Miss Worthington. I'm just not convinced *you* do."

He stares at the gun in your hand. "Do you want me to prove it to you?"

"Yes!" Finally! "I know about the mole Ziggurat has on his neck. Take off your scarf and let me see it!"

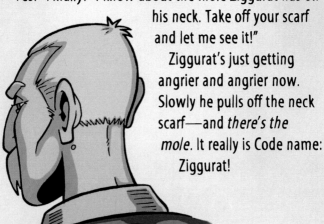

Ziggurat's just getting angrier and angrier now. Slowly he pulls off the neck scarf—and *there's the mole.* It really is Code name: Ziggurat!

GO ON TO THE NEXT PAGE.

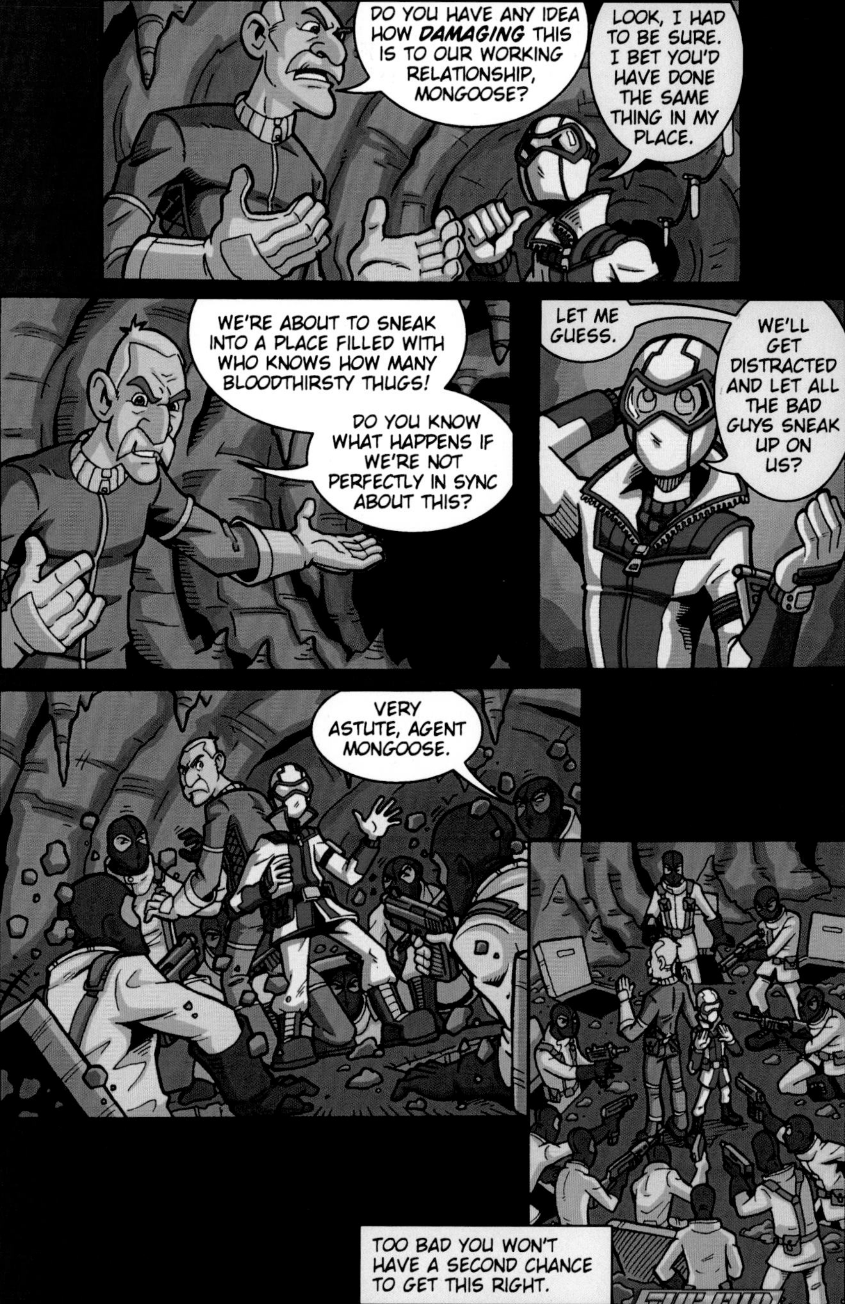
DO YOU HAVE ANY IDEA HOW **DAMAGING** THIS IS TO OUR WORKING RELATIONSHIP, MONGOOSE?
LOOK, I HAD TO BE SURE. I BET YOU'D HAVE DONE THE SAME THING IN MY PLACE.
WE'RE ABOUT TO SNEAK INTO A PLACE FILLED WITH WHO KNOWS HOW MANY BLOODTHIRSTY THUGS!
DO YOU KNOW WHAT HAPPENS IF WE'RE NOT PERFECTLY IN SYNC ABOUT THIS?
LET ME GUESS.
WE'LL GET DISTRACTED AND LET ALL THE BAD GUYS SNEAK UP ON US?
VERY ASTUTE, AGENT MONGOOSE.
TOO BAD YOU WON'T HAVE A SECOND CHANCE TO GET THIS RIGHT.
THE END

"Let's figure out this monster thing first," you whisper to Dolph and Eva. They nod their heads silently. The three of you creep down the dark, damp, smelly passageway. You can hear the grunts getting louder as you go.

Then you turn a corner and see a large chamber ahead of you. Standing in the middle is an *enormous* man—a man you recognize immediately! It's Alexander Wing, one of Van Horst's senior men. All the grunting is because Wing is loading metal crates with . . .

. . . You can't believe it! He's loading them with *gold bars!*

"He must have robbed the national treasury," you say softly.

"I don't know *what* he robbed," Dolph murmurs. "But there's no way those bars are his."

"We have to stop him," Eva whispers. "But Wing is incredibly dangerous. Mongoose, how do you want to handle this?"

GO ON TO THE NEXT PAGE.

You know how strong and how vicious
Wing is supposed to be.

WILL YOU . . .

. . . rush into the room and hope the three
of you can dogpile him?
TURN TO PAGE 57.

. . . try to seal Wing into the room
and avoid fighting him altogether?
TURN TO PAGE 111.

AS DANGEROUS AS ZIGGURAT IS, YOU KNOW YOU CAN'T TAKE ANY CHANCES WITH HIM.

ONE WELL-PLACED NERVE STRIKE AND HE'S OUT FOR THE COUNT.

BUT TAKING CARE OF *HIM* HAS LEFT YOU OPEN TO *HER*.

YOU HURT MY SWEETIE!

NOBODY HURTS MY SWEETIE!

YOU FIGURE, AFTER THIS, IN MISS WORTHINGTON'S FILES UNDER "MARTINIQUE STONE" IT'LL SAY, "VICIOUS, COLD-BLOODED KILLER."

NOT THAT THAT'LL DO *YOU* ANY GOOD.

THE END

Traitor or not, you can't afford to take the chance. As the two of them get closer, your mind races, trying to come up with a plan.

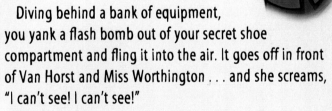

The lights of one of Van Horst's devices glint off Miss Worthington's dark glasses . . . and you have an idea. It's a long shot, but it might work!

Diving behind a bank of equipment, you yank a flash bomb out of your secret shoe compartment and fling it into the air. It goes off in front of Van Horst and Miss Worthington . . . and she screams, "I can't see! I can't see!"

Those shades aren't just for show. She really is sensitive to light!

Van Horst is just distracted enough for you to sneak up behind him and clobber him . . . then you tie the two of them together. "Curse you, Mongoose!" Miss Worthington shouts.

But you're not listening.

You're already picturing a nice, long vacation.

THE END

You agree that it would be best to block the entrance to the tunnel. Creature or no creature, you don't want to be surprised by a sneak attack. Dolph takes a big door from another room and seals it across the tunnel entrance, fixing it in place with a superheated welding laser concealed in his sunglasses.

"Okay," you say, "we should search the cathedral now. Do we start with the upstairs or the downstairs?"

"Downstairs," Eva says at the same time Dolph says, "Upstairs, of course." They start arguing, and it gets heated pretty quickly. Weren't these two supposed to be partners?

"You'll have to settle it, Mongoose," Eva finally says. "Do you agree with me, that we go down, or with this big dolt, that we go up?"

GO ON TO THE NEXT PAGE.

TWISTED JOURNEYS®

You're not too impressed with either Dolph or Eva right now, but you do need to make a choice.

WILL YOU . . .

. . . agree with Dolph and head upstairs?
TURN TO PAGE 93.

. . . go along with Eva and head downstairs?
TURN TO PAGE 50.

YOU'RE ASTOUNDED BY ALL THE GADGETS AND GIZMOS AND THINGAMABOBS IN THIS PLACE. YOU WONDER IF THEY ALL ACTUALLY WORK.

GEE WHIZ. VAN HORST SHOULD HAVE A YARD SALE.

OH! HEY, ARE YOU ALL RIGHT?

LET ME GET YOU OUT OF THOSE...

If Ziggurat is a double agent, you can't take any chances with him.

He never sees your kick coming—you hit him on the back of the knee and knock him down. Then you clamp your arms around his neck. You know he'll be unconscious in just a few seconds this way.

But you've misjudged him! He's *way* stronger than you thought!

He breaks free and growls as he turns to face you. "So that's how it is!" he whispers. "Van Horst has sent a double agent after me! Well, Miss Worthington will promote me when she sees how I've dealt with you . . . and I'll use the trophy I took off the *last* Van Horst spy to do it!"

You realize you've made a terrible mistake, but Ziggurat's not giving you the chance to explain. He whips out the Van Horst knife . . . and that's the last thing you see . . .

THE END

"Look, Ziggurat, you've got to talk to her," you tell him. "If she really loves you, then she'll come back with us. Miss Worthington won't punish her—or you—if Martinique comes over to our side."

He seems uncertain. "Really? You think so?"

You nod. "You should go talk to her."

Ziggurat goes and speaks to Martinique Stone. He wasn't lying—she gives him a hug and kiss when she sees him. They talk for a few minutes. Then they come back to you, hand in hand.

"I hope you're right," she says to you. "Van Horst looks dimly on turncoats."

"Don't worry," you reply. "Let's just set the explosive charges, then we'll take off."

With the Arctic facility nothing more than a smoking crater now, Martinique Stone gets a warm welcome from Miss Worthington—and you get a promotion! You guess Van Horst himself will have to wait for another assignment . . .

THE END

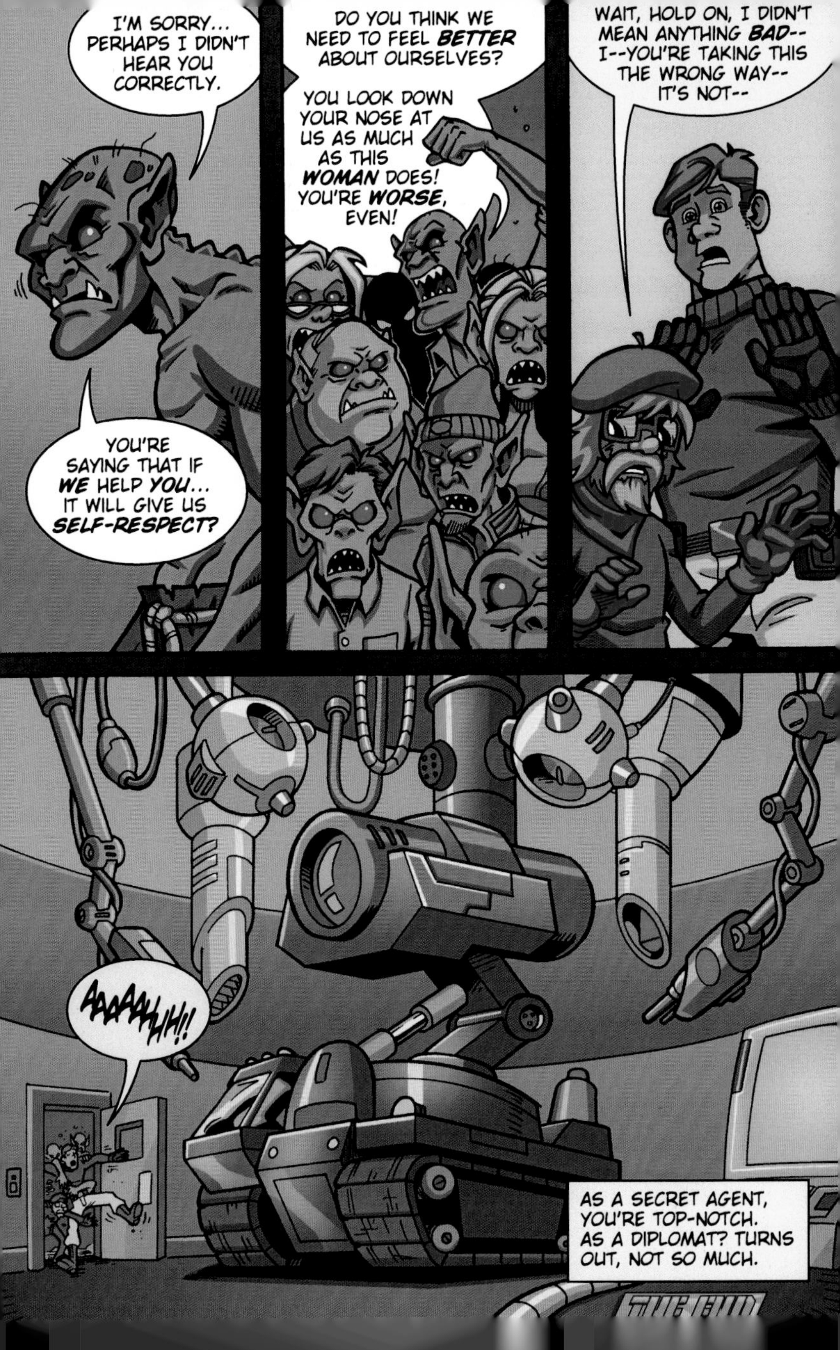
I'M SORRY... PERHAPS I DIDN'T HEAR YOU CORRECTLY.
YOU'RE SAYING THAT IF WE HELP YOU... IT WILL GIVE US SELF-RESPECT?
DO YOU THINK WE NEED TO FEEL BETTER ABOUT OURSELVES?
YOU LOOK DOWN YOUR NOSE AT US AS MUCH AS THIS WOMAN DOES! YOU'RE WORSE, EVEN!
WAIT, HOLD ON, I DIDN'T MEAN ANYTHING BAD-- I--YOU'RE TAKING THIS THE WRONG WAY-- IT'S NOT--
AAAAAHHH!!
AS A SECRET AGENT, YOU'RE TOP-NOTCH. AS A DIPLOMAT? TURNS OUT, NOT SO MUCH.

You have to go with your gut. Even though he helped you complete the assignment, there's something about Ziggurat that doesn't seem right.

He frowns at you. "You *still* don't trust me, do you?"

"I have to be sure. Tell me: what's Miss Worthington's middle name?"

Your partner stares at you for a long minute—and then reaches up and pulls off the latex Ziggurat mask he was wearing, mole and all! Suddenly you're face-to-face with *Franklin da Silva*.

"You couldn't leave well enough alone, could you?" he asks, sneering. "Well, no matter. I'm taking *over*. This was just the first step."

But you were already suspicious. And now that he's revealed himself . . .

. . . you fire the mini-Taser you had concealed in your palm. He never sees it coming.

Maybe you didn't get Van Horst himself today. But destroying his device *and* capturing his lieutenant? That's a pain that'll linger!

THE END

82

SOMETIMES YOUR SENSE OF ADVENTURE GETS THE BEST OF YOU. A *CREATURE?* OF *COURSE* YOU HAVE TO INVESTIGATE IT!

BESIDES, YOU CAN'T HAVE SOME HUGE, UNKNOWN THING RUNNING AROUND DOWN HERE, MAYBE EVEN INTERFERING WITH YOUR OPERATION.

SOONER THAN ANY OF YOU EXPECTED, YOU *DO* HEAR SOUNDS.

HNGH! HRKH! HNGH!

WHILE FROM THE OTHER DIRECTION, VERY, VERY FAINTLY, YOU THINK YOU CAN HEAR SOMEONE CRYING OUT FOR *HELP.*

MONGOOSE? YOU'RE IN CHARGE HERE. WHAT SHOULD WE DO?

GO ON TO THE NEXT PAGE

You wanted to go after the creature
and you think you hear it . . . but it's
hard to ignore cries for help!

WILL YOU . . .

. . . follow your new agenda and track
this "monster" down?
TURN TO PAGE 72.

. . . see if you can help whoever's
crying out?
TURN TO PAGE 14.

"Ziggurat," you whisper, "your loyalty has been compromised. You know that. You can't go on as an active agent."

He frowns at you. "What are you saying?"

"I'm saying you need to turn yourself in. If you do it willingly and cooperate, I'm sure Miss Worthington will go easy on you."

"Turn myself in?" His frown gets darker. "But I'd lose everything! *Everything!* My job, my one true love . . . my whole life!"

"It's the right thing to do," you tell him calmly. "And you know it."

"Okay, okay, give me a minute to think, all right?" He steps away . . .

. . . and then he smashes open the lock on the chain around the barrels, sending the entire huge stack tumbling down, straight at you!

Just before the rumbling, crushing weight falls on you, you hear him say, "Sorry. Guess I have some issues with the whole 'right and wrong' thing."

THE END

"The woman I work for is the head of a very powerful agency," you tell the creatures' leader. "A very *rich* agency, to be honest. She can give you a handsome reward if you help us."

Eva screams, "Don't listen to this nonsense! You need to do what I tell you to do! You know what happens if I get angry!"

But the creatures don't seem to hear her. Their leader tells you, "All we have ever wanted was to be treated fairly." He turns and sniffs in Eva's direction. "And now we begin to understand that fair treatment is *not* what this one has offered us."

GO ON TO THE NEXT PAGE.

WAIT! NO! **WAIT!!**

A COUPLE OF MINUTES LATER...

NOW, I BELIEVE WE WERE DISCUSSING WHAT SORT OF COMPENSATION WE MIGHT GET FOR HELPING YOU?

NO PROBLEM!

HERE, LET ME SHOW YOU THE HIDDEN ELEVATOR TO THE EMP ROOM.

YOU FEEL PRETTY SAFE IN SAYING YOU'LL GET YOUR NEW FRIENDS **WHATEVER** THEY **WANT!**

The little robots are all around you, shooting, stinging. With all your strength, you kick Van Horst's hand until he lets go of your ankle. Then you do the only thing you can think of . . .

. . . which is to fling your body out in a kind of sideways somersault, your hands gripping the ladder. Your feet whip around in a brutal arc and smash two of the robots into each other. They fall to the floor, destroyed.

Planting your feet again, you grab the third robot right out of the air and aim its laser beam at Van Horst's hand. Van Horst gives a startled yelp and loses his grip on the ladder . . .

. . . and you watch as he plummets to the hard metal plating, far below.

You've finally defeated Van Horst!

Of course, his henchmen are still out there . . . and will probably carry on his evil ways.

But that's something to deal with another day.

THE END

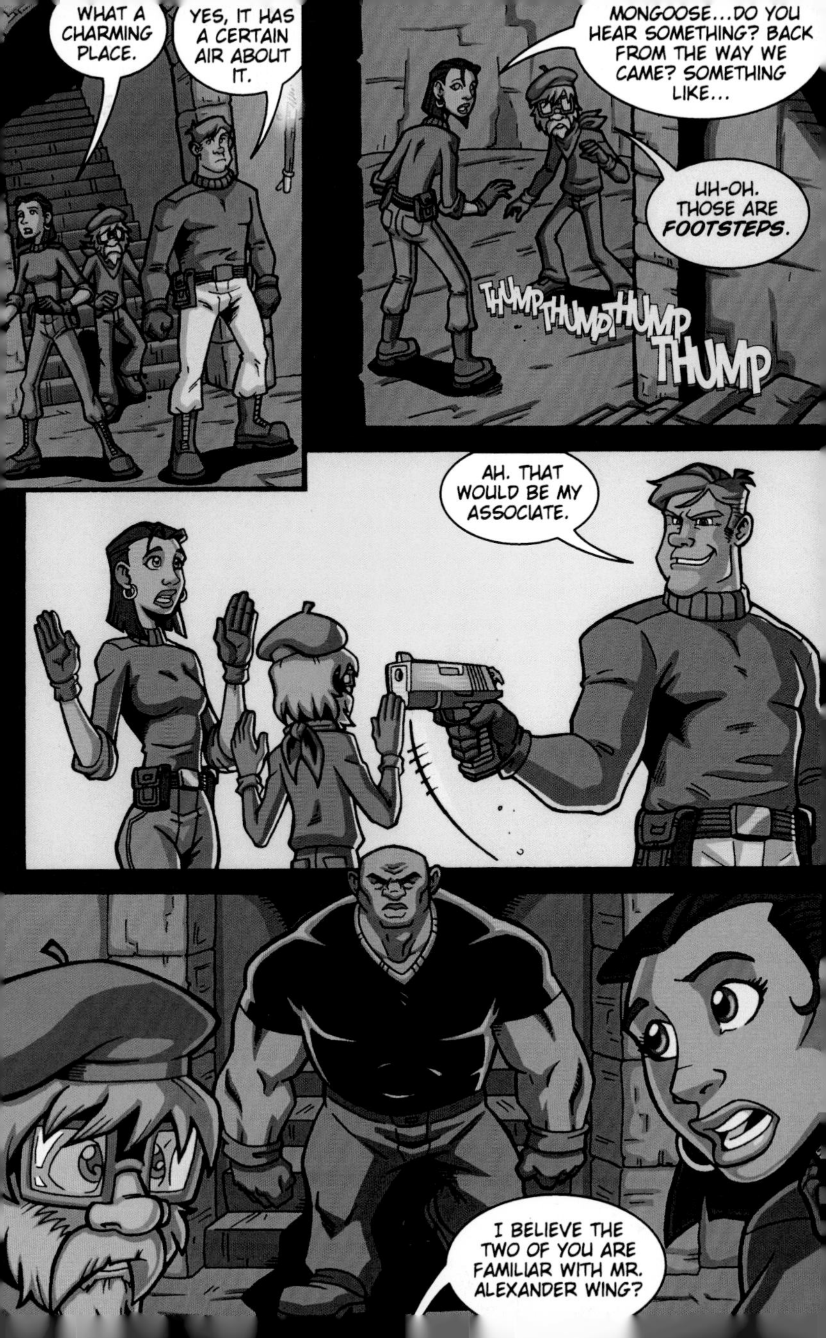
WHAT A CHARMING PLACE.
YES, IT HAS A CERTAIN AIR ABOUT IT.
MONGOOSE...DO YOU HEAR SOMETHING? BACK FROM THE WAY WE CAME? SOMETHING LIKE...
UH-OH. THOSE ARE *FOOTSTEPS*.
THUMP THUMP THUMP THUMP
AH. THAT WOULD BE MY ASSOCIATE.
I BELIEVE THE TWO OF YOU ARE FAMILIAR WITH MR. ALEXANDER WING?

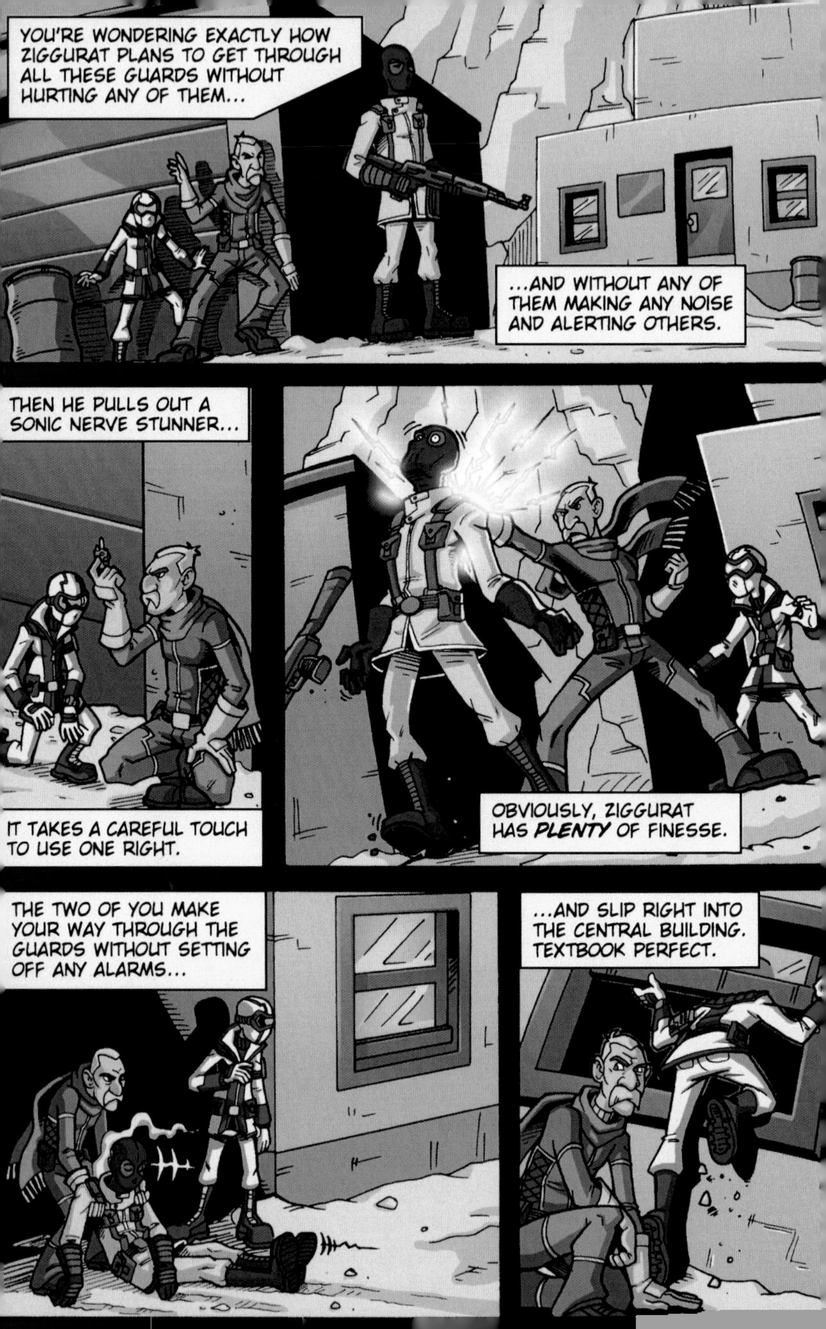
YOU'RE WONDERING EXACTLY HOW ZIGGURAT PLANS TO GET THROUGH ALL THESE GUARDS WITHOUT HURTING ANY OF THEM...
...AND WITHOUT ANY OF THEM MAKING ANY NOISE AND ALERTING OTHERS.
THEN HE PULLS OUT A SONIC NERVE STUNNER...
IT TAKES A CAREFUL TOUCH TO USE ONE RIGHT.
OBVIOUSLY, ZIGGURAT HAS *PLENTY* OF FINESSE.
THE TWO OF YOU MAKE YOUR WAY THROUGH THE GUARDS WITHOUT SETTING OFF ANY ALARMS...
...AND SLIP RIGHT INTO THE CENTRAL BUILDING. TEXTBOOK PERFECT.

Inside the building, you find yourselves at the corner of an L-shaped hallway. At one end, you can see a big room packed with super-high-tech equipment. You're certain that's the research lab you're looking for.

But at the other end . . . through a doorway . . . you can see Martinique Stone! She's one of Van Horst's ultra-dangerous lieutenants—and you don't think she knows you're there yet.

It would look *so* good on your record if you captured her. Not only that, but it would also make sense to neutralize her, so that she doesn't interrupt you while you're analyzing all the hypno-beam equipment.

"Never mind her," Ziggurat whispers. "Let's get our goal accomplished! That's our objective, first and foremost. We can worry about other things later."

GO ON TO THE NEXT PAGE.

Ziggurat's right—dealing with the hypno-beam equipment *is* your primary objective. But if you don't nab Martinique Stone right now, she could get away—or worse!

WILL YOU . . .

. . . decide to hold off on the equipment until you've made sure Stone is not a threat?
TURN TO PAGE 54.

. . . ignore Stone and go for the equipment?
TURN TO PAGE 102.

"I think we should go up and then work our way down," you say, after some thought.

Dolph folds his arms across his chest and looks smug. Eva scowls at you both. "I thought you had better sense than that, Mongoose," she practically hisses. "But whatever. If you really want to go upstairs, I'll bow to the majority opinion."

Dolph leads the way. The stairs groan and creak under his weight, but they hold together. Soon you all emerge into a long hallway with rooms opening off it along the right side.

"One at a time," you whisper. They both nod. Together you move into the first room . . .

. . . and you frown as Dolph pushes the door closed behind him and latches it.

GO ON TO THE NEXT PAGE.

DOLPH? WHAT ARE YOU DOING? WHY DID YOU LOCK THE DOOR?

SIMPLE.

I DIDN'T WANT EITHER OF YOU RUNNING OFF SOMEPLACE...

...WHERE I COULDN'T SEE THE *LOOKS* ON YOUR FACES WHEN I REVEAL WHO I REALLY AM.

DR. SANTIAGO VAN HORST, AT YOUR SERVICE.

You and Eva fan out, trying to get on opposite sides of Van Horst. He can't watch you both, right? Maybe one of you can get in a lucky shot.

But Van Horst doesn't seem concerned at all. "You can forget about using any of your little gadgets on me," he growls. "No knockout gas, no Tasers, no sonic brain-scramblers. I've been making improvements." You're not sure what he means . . .

. . . but then Van Horst pulls off his gloves, revealing *metal hands!* This guy is part *robot?*

"What do we do?" Eva shouts.

"I don't know!" you shout back. "This wasn't part of the training!"

Van Horst laughs, and you realize that being part robot means he can move really, *really* fast. He gets those metal hands on the two of you before you can do anything about it, and before you realize it . . .

. . . everything goes black.

THE END

You and your teammates make your way into the cathedral. The light is dim, and huge shadows seem to flit around everywhere. The building looks and smells incredibly old . . . and you can hear skitters and soft thumping sounds from the walls and ceiling. *Is that just because the place is so old?* you wonder. *Or is there something in the walls making those sounds?*

You go through a door into a different section of the cathedral and find yourself looking at a wooden staircase that goes both up through the ceiling and down through the floor.

Dolph frowns. "Is that . . . some kind of machinery I'm hearing?"

You and Eva listen. If you concentrate, you can hear it too: a low, mechanical hum. But you can't tell if it's coming from upstairs or downstairs.

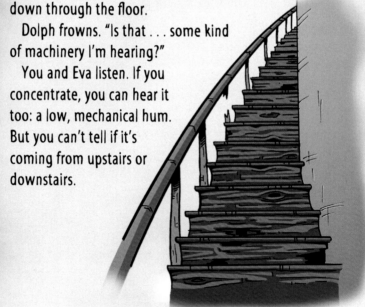

GO ON TO THE NEXT PAGE.

TWISTED JOURNEYS®

The mechanical sound has to be the EMP equipment Van Horst is researching! That staircase looks pretty rickety and unsafe, though. On the other hand, the last place you want to go is the basement of a dark, foul-smelling old building.

WILL YOU . . .

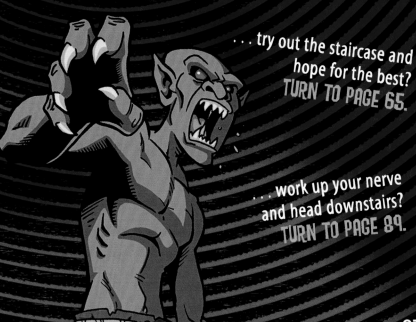

. . . try out the staircase and hope for the best?
TURN TO PAGE 65.

. . . work up your nerve and head downstairs?
TURN TO PAGE 89.

You and Ziggurat don't speak again, and he only gives you a single nod as you leave. You feel pretty good about the assignment. After all, you did blow up Van Horst's machine. Still, you're afraid you *were* too suspicious.

Then, two days later, you get called into Miss Worthington's office—and there's Ziggurat, standing right next to her, both of them eyeballing you! He must have turned in a complaint!

"Ziggurat has filed a formal statement with this office," Miss Worthington says, and your stomach tightens up. Will you get suspended? Even fired . . . ?

"Yes?" you respond. Your voice only shakes a little.

"Yes." She stands . . . and shakes your hand! "He has decided that your instincts were right on target and that he would have done the same thing in your position. Congratulations, Mongoose. Agent Ziggurat will now be your official partner."

Partner? Well . . . that's sort of a happy ending . . . Right?

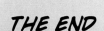

THE END

MIGHT AS WELL SEE WHAT'S DOWN HERE.

WOW...

LOOKS AS THOUGH VAN HORST HAS BEEN EXPERIMENTING WITH DIFFERENT ECOSYSTEMS DOWN HERE!

TROPICAL

DESERT

TECHNOLOGY

"DESERT" AND "TROPICAL" SEEM PRETTY STRAIGHTFORWARD. YOU'RE NOT SURE EXACTLY WHAT YOU'LL FIND IN "TECHNOLOGY."

You know Van Horst is going to come after you, so you've got to make a quick decision.

WILL YOU . . .

. . . explore the tropical dome?
TURN TO PAGE 8.

. . . check out the desert dome?
TURN TO PAGE 12.

. . . see what's in the tech dome?
TURN TO PAGE 78.

"Sorry, Ziggurat," you say as you pull your gun on him. "I need you to turn and put both your hands on the wall."

"What are you doing?" he whispers fiercely. "I'm on your side!"

"No, you're on your *own* side. You can't be loyal to Miss Worthington *and* to Martinique Stone."

"You're making a big mistake," he tells you as you click your handcuffs on his left wrist.

"I have no choice."

Then you feel the point of a knife on the back of your neck. "Sure you do," Martinique Stone breathes into your ear. She snuck up on you while you were dealing with Ziggurat!

"You okay, honey?" she asks Ziggurat sweetly.

"I will be," he says, turning to face you, "as soon as we deal with this kid."

Looks as if Ziggurat's made his choice. Too bad . . .

. . . for you.

THE END

ZIGGURAT'S SUSPICIOUS BEHAVIOR ASIDE, HE'S BEEN GREAT TO WORK WITH SO FAR ON THIS MISSION.

BUT THEN...

...ZIGGURAT PROVES HE'S WORTH HIS WEIGHT IN *GOLD*.

WOW...YOU REALLY SAVED MY BACON. THANK YOU.

JUST DOING MY JOB.

COME ON, LET'S GET ON WITH IT.

You and Ziggurat creep into the hypno-beam lab, document everything in there, and take as many pictures as the memory chips in your cameras can hold. Then you plant twenty tiny explosive charges—just enough to wreck the machines without hurting any of the people around.

On your way out you try to go after Martinique Stone, but there's no sign of her. Maybe she caught wind of you, or maybe she simply left. Either way, you and your partner make it back to the safety of the ice cave. Ziggurat pulls out a signaling device and hits a button. You can *just* make out the muffled explosions.

"Well done, kid," Ziggurat says as you head back toward the airstrip. "We've saved the day."

"Yeah," you reply. "But Van Horst and his goons are still out there."

Ziggurat shrugs. "We'll find them some other time."

Ziggurat's right. You *will* find them—even if it takes the rest of your life.

THE END

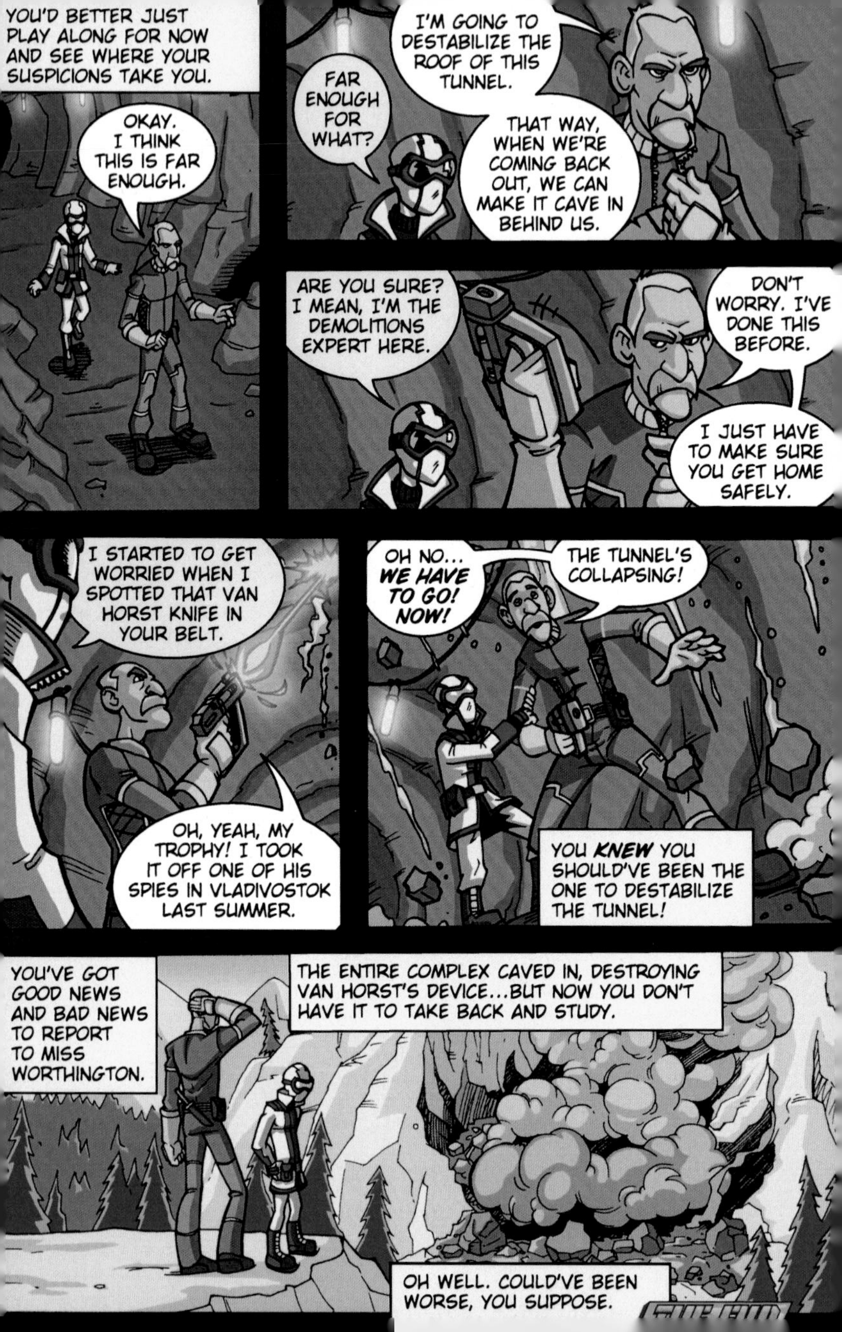
YOU'D BETTER JUST PLAY ALONG FOR NOW AND SEE WHERE YOUR SUSPICIONS TAKE YOU.
OKAY. I THINK THIS IS FAR ENOUGH.
FAR ENOUGH FOR WHAT?
I'M GOING TO DESTABILIZE THE ROOF OF THIS TUNNEL.
THAT WAY, WHEN WE'RE COMING BACK OUT, WE CAN MAKE IT CAVE IN BEHIND US.
ARE YOU SURE? I MEAN, I'M THE DEMOLITIONS EXPERT HERE.
DON'T WORRY. I'VE DONE THIS BEFORE.
I JUST HAVE TO MAKE SURE YOU GET HOME SAFELY.
I STARTED TO GET WORRIED WHEN I SPOTTED THAT VAN HORST KNIFE IN YOUR BELT.
OH, YEAH, MY TROPHY! I TOOK IT OFF ONE OF HIS SPIES IN VLADIVOSTOK LAST SUMMER.
OH NO... *WE HAVE TO GO! NOW!*
THE TUNNEL'S COLLAPSING!
YOU ***KNEW*** YOU SHOULD'VE BEEN THE ONE TO DESTABILIZE THE TUNNEL!
YOU'VE GOT GOOD NEWS AND BAD NEWS TO REPORT TO MISS WORTHINGTON.
THE ENTIRE COMPLEX CAVED IN, DESTROYING VAN HORST'S DEVICE...BUT NOW YOU DON'T HAVE IT TO TAKE BACK AND STUDY.
OH WELL. COULD'VE BEEN WORSE, YOU SUPPOSE.

You just know Miss Worthington couldn't be a traitor! She *has* to be working undercover. You catch her eye and very subtly indicate the floor hatch. You hope she gets your message: *Let's head toward that hatch and try to get away from Van Horst together.*

"So what's it going to be, Mongoose?" Van Horst asks you. He sounds really smug. "Are you going to try to fight? Or will we finally see the famous secret agent surrender?"

"Neither!" you shout, as you spring toward the floor hatch. If Miss Worthington can just provide a little bit of distraction, you can both get away!

But what Miss Worthington provides is a shot from a high-voltage Taser gun, right in the back of your neck. As you fall to the floor, your vision getting dark, you *still* can't believe it.

Until she speaks to you.

"Sorry, Mongoose," she says. "You're fired."

THE END

The three of you make your way down a long, foul-smelling tunnel. Moss of some kind grows between the rocks under your feet. You have to be careful not to slip and fall.

"So you're the great Code name: Mongoose," Eva says quietly.

You shrug. "I don't know that I'd say 'great.'"

"There's no need for false modesty," she tells you. "Your exploits are known throughout the espionage community. What you did in Johannesburg—no one else could have done that."

You're a little embarrassed. You were just doing your job, after all. "Yes, well, thank you, but we should focus on our primary goal now, don't you think?"

Eva smiles sweetly. "Whatever you say, Mongoose."

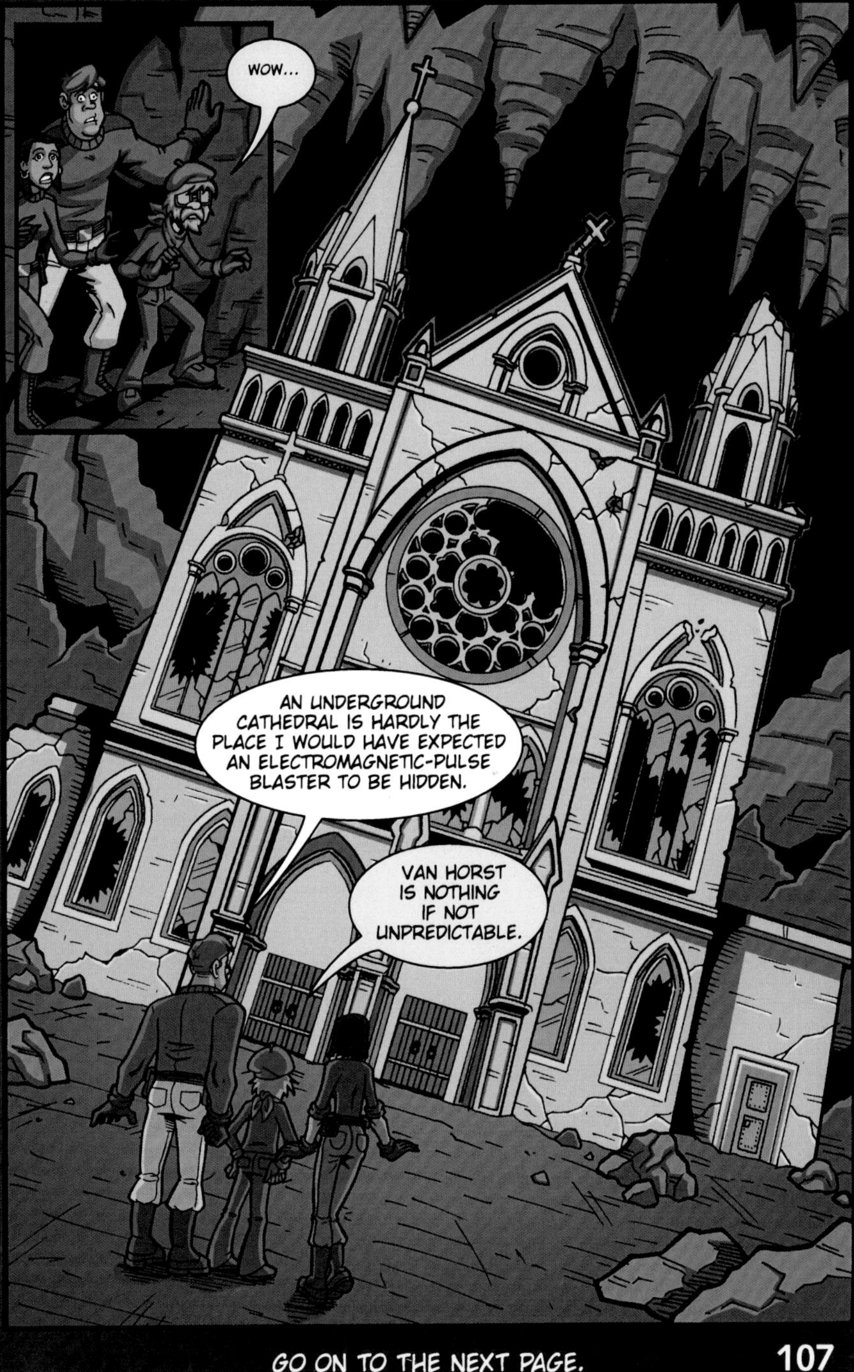
WOW...
AN UNDERGROUND CATHEDRAL IS HARDLY THE PLACE I WOULD HAVE EXPECTED AN ELECTROMAGNETIC-PULSE BLASTER TO BE HIDDEN.
VAN HORST IS NOTHING IF NOT UNPREDICTABLE.

GO ON TO THE NEXT PAGE.

This whole place gives you the creeps. You're not sure what's down here with you or even exactly where to look for what you need to find.

WILL YOU . . .

. . . waste no time and start looking around the cathedral?
TURN TO PAGE 96.

. . . suggest blocking off the hallway you came through, so nothing sneaks up on you?
TURN TO PAGE 76.

. . . point out that metal door off to the side and start looking there first?
TURN TO PAGE 37.

You think there's something familiar about the person on the floor. "Hold on," you say. "I'll have you free in a second or two."

The hooded head lifts, and a voice you'd recognize anywhere comes out of it. "Mongoose? Is that you?"

"Miss Worthington!" you cry. You pull the hood off your boss's head—then you straighten her dark glasses, which got knocked askew under the hood. "What are you doing here?"

"Van Horst kidnapped me," she says shortly. "Or was that not obvious?" You get the handcuffs off her wrists and help her into her jacket.

"So what do you want to do now?" you ask. She *is* your boss, after all.

"I should think it would be clear," she replies. "We find Van Horst. And we neutralize him."

GO ON TO THE NEXT PAGE.

You and Miss Worthington head back to the main dome, and the way the two of you are walking, you half expect heroic theme music to play. It's at that point that you remember that Miss Worthington was a secret agent, just like you, long before she took the desk job she has now.

"Van Horst!" she shouts when you enter the dome. "Get out here!"

Your arch-nemesis saunters out to the middle of the floor. "What's this?" he asks. "A woman and a little kid are going to beat *me*?"

But Miss Worthington doesn't even give him the chance to say another word. She screams and charges, and you're right there next to her—and the two of you fight together really well, as it turns out! Van Horst is flattened within ten seconds.

"Well done, Mongoose," she says, dusting off her hands. "I'd say this case is officially closed."

THE END

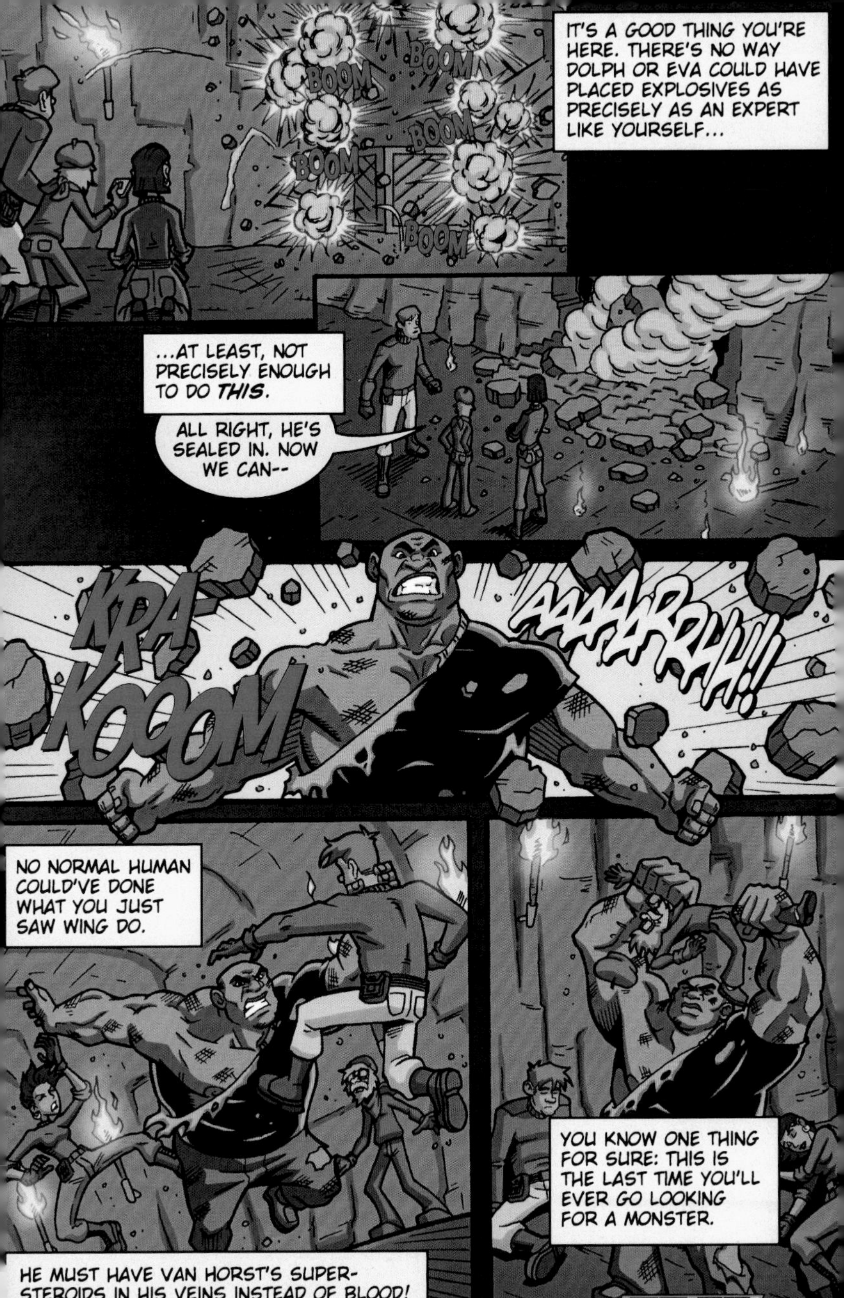
BOOM
BOOM
BOOM
BOOM
BOOM
IT'S A GOOD THING YOU'RE HERE. THERE'S NO WAY DOLPH OR EVA COULD HAVE PLACED EXPLOSIVES AS PRECISELY AS AN EXPERT LIKE YOURSELF...
...AT LEAST, NOT PRECISELY ENOUGH TO DO *THIS*.
ALL RIGHT, HE'S SEALED IN. NOW WE CAN--
KRA-KOOOM
AAAARRHH!!
NO NORMAL HUMAN COULD'VE DONE WHAT YOU JUST SAW WING DO.
HE MUST HAVE VAN HORST'S SUPER-STEROIDS IN HIS VEINS INSTEAD OF BLOOD!
YOU KNOW ONE THING FOR SURE: THIS IS THE LAST TIME YOU'LL EVER GO LOOKING FOR A MONSTER.

WHICH TWISTED JOURNEYS® WILL YOU TRY NEXT?

#1 CAPTURED BY PIRATES
Can you keep a band of scurvy pirates from turning you into shark bait?

#2 ESCAPE FROM PYRAMID X
Not every ancient mummy stays dead . . .

#3 TERROR IN GHOST MANSION
The spooks in this Halloween house aren't wearing costumes . . .

#4 THE TREASURE OF MOUNT FATE
Can you survive monsters and magic and bring home the treasure?

#5 NIGHTMARE ON ZOMBIE ISLAND
Will you be the first to escape Zombie Island?

#6 THE TIME TRAVEL TRAP
Danger is everywhere when you're caught in a time machine!

#7 VAMPIRE HUNT
Vampire hunters are creeping through an ancient castle. And you're the vampire they're hunting!

#8 ALIEN INCIDENT ON PLANET J
Make peace with the Makaknuk, Zirifubi, and Frongo, or you'll never get off their planet . . .

#9 AGENT MONGOOSE AND THE HYPNO-BEAM SCHEME
Your top-secret mission, if you choose to accept it: foil the plots of an evil mastermind!

#10 THE GOBLIN KING
Will you join the fearsome goblins or the dangerous elves?